Smooth As Whiskey
Tiffany Casper

As If...

Book 3

Copyright © Tiffany Casper 2024

All rights reserved. No part of this publication may be reproduced, distributed, or transmitted in any form or by any means, including photocopying, recording, or other electronic or mechanical methods, without the prior written permission of the publisher, except in the case of brief quotations embodied in critical reviews and certain other noncommercial uses permitted by copyright law.

Any references to historical events, real people, or real places are used fictitiously. Names, characters, and places are products of the author's imagination.

Acknowledgments
Cover Designer: Tiffany Casper

Billie, Tami, Raylene, Chrystal, and Elaine, my rock-hard team.

Synopsis

Club girls never get their happily ever after.

It was a known fact.

However, for the men of Zagan MC, they didn't give a damn.

Only they didn't realize the battle that they would need to win.

Their hearts.

Because a girl didn't wake up and declare she was going to be a Club Girl.

This is Sutton & Irish's story.

Song

Chasing After You – Ryan Hurd Ft. Maren Morris

Zagan MC

Asher – President

Whit – Vice President

Priest – Enforcer

Creature – Enforcer

Rome – SGT at Arms

Pipe – Secretary

Irish – Road Captain

Trigger – Treasurer

Charlie – Tech

Coal – Icer

Table of Contents

Smooth As Whiskey
Copyright © Tiffany Casper 2024
Acknowledgments
Synopsis
Song
Zagan MC
Table of Contents
Prologue
Chapter 1
Chapter 2
Chapter 3
Chapter 4
Chapter 5
Chapter 6
Chapter 7
Chapter 8
Chapter 9
Chapter 10
Chapter 11
Chapter 12
Chapter 13

Chapter 14
Epilogue
Thank You
Other Works

Prologue
Sutton

With my butt at the base of the tree, I hunkered in for a long-ass night.

The fourth long-ass night I would be spending with animals that made the forest their home.

Normally, I would try to find somewhere that would offer me adequate coverage. But there was no way I was going to be able to walk another couple of miles.

Much less another couple of feet.

Not after everything I had endured and not after I had pushed my body well past its limits.

Luckily, this tree had some thick leaves and low-hanging branches, so it offered a dry spot.

Just as I settled in and thanked the heavens for the dry spot, that was when the rain that everyone had been talking about for the past week hit.

Big fat raindrops poured down.

The sounds of them hitting the leaves.

Little critters doing the same thing I was, trying to get to a dry place.

I knew I was safe, at least for tonight.

Because no way was that man going to be caught out in this and risk getting his shoes ruined.

Oh no. Not Raymond Frederick Stanton IV.

Him and his Italian loafers.

His pants that had to be dry-cleaned.

His shirt that was never allowed to bore a single wrinkle.

The vest he wore always had to be pressed.

And don't even get me started on the cufflinks.

Oh, what the hell.

I needed something to keep my mind off the cold that was going to hit my bones here in just a few short hours.

His cufflinks? I had to clean them all every morning and wear white gloves when I held them.

Because heaven forbid, I leave a single fingerprint on them or even a little speck of dust.

Trust me, I made sure I cleaned those bad boys within an inch of their lives.

Feeling the back of someone's hand, well, you learned quickly to make things work so you don't ever have to feel that again.

Or, at the very least, you freaking tried to.

Now, are you asking why I have put up with his stuff for so long?

Simple.

He held the one thing I treasured most in this world in the palm of his hand.

The one thing my mama gave me before she died.

A beautiful ruby red tennis bracelet that my father had saved up every penny he could to buy for her before he deployed.

And he had planned to make my mother his wife when he got back.

Only... he left the world behind with that bracelet, and me still inside my mother's womb.

Why did Raymond Frederick Stanton IV have it, you ask?

Well, that was quite simple. He married my mother when I was nine and won her over because she had told him no on a date.

So, like all assholes with a micro-sized penis when their egos get bruised, he made it his mission to get my mother.

Did he punish her for the three years they were married for telling him no? Yes.

If I say he was the best thing that ever could have happened to my mother, I would be a liar.

A straight-up, no-holds-barred liar.

So, why was he holding my mother's bracelet over my head?

Simple. With her gone, he couldn't use me to make her do the things I knew she didn't want to do.

Because I was that amazing lady's one weakness.

And she was that, an amazing lady.

I could go on and on about her, but unfortunately, I needed to stay vigilant.

I needed to stay vigilant because even though Raymond Frederick IV would never be caught dead out here unless he was glamping in a five-star resort... that didn't mean he didn't have men that he could send after me.

And he did.

And because of one man he had working for him... after the conversation I heard in his study... well... needless to say, he could keep that bracelet for all I cared.

Well, I used the word keep, extremely loosely. He could borrow it until I found a way to get it back.

And I would get it back, even if it was the last thing in this world I would ever do.

But first, I had to make sure I always stayed one step ahead of him and his men. Sadly, I didn't know how to go about that when all I was able to take with me were the clothes on my back and nothing else.

And the little material I wore... well, it was torn in places. I would get to that part of the story in a moment.

Why did I decide it was time to flee?

That centered around the heinous crime that took place in his study... minutes... hours before I fled.

He had guards posted up around the house, which was normal for him, but the number of guards he had stationed was to make sure that I didn't leave the house.

Apparently, he had a wealthy businessman coming to the house, and we were getting married that night. A man I had met before when he came to the house. A man who had a wandering eye. And wrinkled hands.

But not before he *gifted* me to the meanest son of a bitch I had ever met.

Gerard was his name.

And he made Freddy Kruger look like he was nothing but a happy fairy. Going merrily on his way.

He was cold. So cold it was a wonder that the room he held in my stepfather's house wasn't made of anything but ice.

Ice that never thawed even on the hottest day of the year in Mississippi, which could reach one hundred and seven degrees.

The man he was marrying me to wasn't much better.

Still, if I had to choose, I would have chosen him over Gerard any day of the week.

Hell, I would choose to marry the worst criminal known throughout history over Gerard.

Especially after the heinous crime he had committed against me once the word gifting had fallen from Raymond Frederick Stanton IV's mouth.

The most important thing you can do if you are no match for your attacker after you've said the word no so many times that your voice is hoarse after you've screamed for someone, anyone, to help you is to retreat as deep into your mind that you could go.

Mine was when my mother and I accidentally added salt instead of sugar to a batch of cookies we made.

But sadly, that memory didn't extend as far as when he pulled out of my battered and bruised body, and Raymond Frederick Stanton IV was still sitting in the same chair when Gerard walked in behind me and locked the door.

I shook my head, trying to get those memories to disappear from my mind for even just a little while.

The man he wanted me to marry... well... he was closing in on fifty. And I was eighteen years old as of four days ago.

I don't mind age differences in people. Ten years? Okay. Fifteen years? Sure. But someone old enough to be my father had he had me at thirty-two? Umm, yeah, no, I'll pass.

It was all so Raymond Frederick Stanton IV could get a new piece of territory that he desperately needed. New territory for what I didn't know.

I also didn't know what he did for work, but I knew that he left every morning at eight twenty-five and returned home around five forty-five, and then he would either stay home while men came to see him, or he would leave with a large contingency of men.

But whatever the reason, I didn't care.

I was eighteen years old... and ever since my mother passed away when I was fifteen, I had been dreading that fateful day.

The day he had been waiting for.

But... what he hadn't known about, and none of his soldiers had surmised, was that I had an ally in the house.

Someone who only worked for him due to a blood debt from her father that she was trying to fulfill.

My heart broke for Rebecca, but sadly, even though we had talked about why she didn't forget about the promise she made to a dying man and leave... Tulane's don't break their promises, she had told me.

And I admired her for that, I really and truly did.

That was the last thought I had before I gritted my teeth, shoved myself closer to the base of the tree I was huddled against, and thought about the warmest place I could muster.

Because I was getting cold.

But what I didn't know... was that everything I had been praying for ever since I stared at the coffin that was lowered into the ground that held my mother was about to come true... or so I thought anyway.

Irish

"Yo!"

Every head in the main room of the clubhouse turned at Charlie's voice.

When he tilted his head to his tablet, Asher, Coal, Whit, Stoney, and I stood up and walked over to where he sat.

"See that?" He was pointing at something huddled against the base of a tree.

It was hard to see it with the rain pelting down in sheets.

I squinted my eyes, trying to make it out.

And when whatever was huddled there shifted, and their face was revealed, I felt something in my gut tighten.

Unlike anything I've ever felt before.

But I was the stupid son of a bitch that ignored that gut feeling.

And I wouldn't know until years later… when I looked in the mirror, I would only have myself to blame.

Chapter 1
Irish
Almost Two Years Later

"Okay, Sutton is two months away from completing her term with us," At Asher's words, I felt every single eye come to me.

And seeing as that was eighteen eyes, I felt fucking naked.

Which was why I popped off, "Why the fuck are y'all looking at me for?"

Priest lifted his brow, "Cause you basically piss a circle around her any time another man gets near her."

I scoffed, "No, I fucking don't."

Right?

Trigger cackled and then said, "Right. That's why you punched the president of the Pagan's Soldiers in the face for daring to run his hand over her ass."

Whit nodded his head, "And that's why you told an Immoral Saints member that Sutton had chlamydia and wasn't starting the antibiotics until dinner time. And you said that to him right as you saw him watching her ass as she swayed back and forth to a Beatles song."

Pipe snickered, "Or the time that guy sidled up to her in Juniper's and asked her for a dance. It was a dance, Irish, not a meet in the back hallway. You grabbed him by his shirt collar and dragged him out the door."

Rome, who rarely spoke to anyone, unlike Creature, who we all missed, said, "Yeah, and when she was going for a coffee with a guy who cuts hair with her. You made up some bullshit excuse that caused her to stay here. And the man would rather bone all of us than get anywhere near Sutton."

I held my hands up, "Okay. Okay. So what? She's a friend. All those assholes are pussies. They couldn't handle a woman like Sutton."

"Well, I wouldn't call Steel a pussy. Fucking ever. That man earned his road name," Asher said from the head of the table.

Okay, he was right. But I wasn't referring to the president of the Pagan's Soldiers with that pussy comment.

Priest followed Asher's statement with one of his own, "Well, since we've never sampled her, we don't know what you mean."

I ran my hand through my hair that needed a trim. Sutton just bought new scissors, so I would have her do it tonight.

"Look, I just meant that they wouldn't take care of the goodness in her. They would hurt her. And I won't fucking have that." I said.

"Like you keep hurting her whenever Cynnamin shows up at the clubhouse?" Stoney asked.

I shrugged, "Me and Cynnamin go way back."

And I would be damned if I divulged what was really going on with me and Cynnamin.

She made me a promise, and I made her one.

And I never break my fucking word.

And yes... I saw Sutton's face every single time Cynnamin showed up at the clubhouse and saw the hurt on her face... but there was nothing I could do about it without going back on my word.

A man was nothing if not for his word.

I also knew that once everything was said and done, Sutton would understand.

Sure, it might pain her a bit to see my arm go around another woman, but Sutton was tough. She was strong.

She was never afraid to speak her mind.

Or had she...

Stoney sighed, "You keep treating her like shit, she's going to slip through your fingers. Mark my fucking words, boy. And when it happens, you won't have anyone to blame but yourself."

And at his words, my mind traveled back to that fateful day when I didn't realize my entire world was sitting right in front of me.

We all poured out of the clubhouse in the pouring rain, heading to the back corner of the property.

It took us at least twenty minutes to get to the spot, but once we did, all I heard were inhales of breath.

She looked so tiny, huddled up against the base of the tree.

She couldn't be more than five foot three, five foot four.

She had long brown or black hair.

And she was covered in varying stages of bruises. Bruises that were visible because her clothes had been torn to shreds.

Asher approached her first.

Then Priest.

Rome.

Charlie.

Whitt.

Coal.

Trigger.

Stoney.

She shirked away from anyone who tried to get near her.

But... not from my touch.

Then I didn't hesitate as I scooped her in my arms, and with my brothers around me, I carried her the whole way and into the clubhouse, where it was warm.

Stoney grabbed her a blanket and covered her up.

Thankfully, after a few minutes, she started to rouse.

And then, when she saw all of us, she started to fight.

I've gotten an elbow to the chin before, and it hurt like a bitch.

But even though hers didn't pack that same punch, something deep inside of me registered the pain as being so much worse.

It took us about three hours to get her to calm down and eat something, and after she had a bath, she said, "I only want to tell this story one time. So, can you get the important people of your MC together?"

But she only looked at me when she said that.

After Sutton gave us all her story, the two of us created a friendship of sorts.

And since she didn't have anywhere else to go, and since we weren't in the habit of tossing women out, she stayed.

Until two months later, after a conversation with Gabb, Lizette, and Adeline, she came to me.

Asked me to take away the memory of his hands and replace them with mine.

When I said I've never made love to a woman, I meant up until I had Sutton's naked body lying in the center of my bed.

She was the most gorgeous creature my eyes had ever beheld.

Which was why, while she was sleeping silently, I crept out of the bedroom

I stalked that son of a bitch, and when I had my hands on him, I then proceeded to recreate every bruise and every scar on her body. But I did it worse.

And I made sure that one of his ribs ruptured his lung.

I followed that by cutting the man's dick off and shoving it down his throat while saying, "I hope you choke on it, you sorry piece of shit."

And I stood there, with my arms crossed on my chest and my head tilted to the side, as I watched his body take failing breaths and then nothing.

Bye. Bye Motherfucker.

Sadly, the fucker Raymond whatever the fuck his name was, was nowhere to be found.

But I would find him.

And when I did...

Bye. Bye Motherfucker.

As we all walked out of church, I heard Sutton laughing from the kitchen.

And at the sound of her laughter, my dick got hard.

And since she was always ready for me, I headed in that direction.

She was standing there, her head thrown back, still laughing, that ashy brown hair reaching her bra strap.

Her eyes were closed.

But I knew beneath those eyelids held the prettiest eyes I had ever seen.

They were a shade of green, but you have to picture the shade just right.

When you walk outside in the early morning hours, just as dawn is about to break over the horizon, when there's dew on the ground, covering the blades of grass, just below the dew is the color of Sutton's eyes.

But what makes them spectacular are the smaller flecks of gold surrounding her pupil.

I came back to my thoughts when I felt eyes on me.

I looked directly at Sutton and crooked my finger at her.

She smiled, then walked over to me, not having to sashay or move any other way.

She was delectable all on her own.

And with that thought, I bent at the waist and tossed her over my shoulder.

Then, I stormed across the main room of the clubhouse and went right to her room.

Her laughter fell freely from her lungs.

And every thought I had in church suddenly vanished when I slid my dick into her welcoming heat.

Chapter 2
Sutton

I laughed at Marjorie, the client's hair I had just set rollers in, "I'm telling you, girlie, you make them fall in love with your taste, and then you talk about a wedding nonstop. They will get the hint. Eventually."

"But what if you don't believe in marriage? Then what?" I asked her.

She looked up at me and snapped, "A beautiful woman like you doesn't believe in marriage? That I don't believe."

I giggled, "I do. But what if I didn't? What would you tell me to do then?"

"You slip arsenic in his food and make it to where he never wants to go anywhere, and then when he's at his most weakened state, you tie that fool to your bed."

I laughed.

Since Marjorie was my last client of the day, and it was a Tuesday, I made plans to grab Imperial and watch the new *Twisters* movie.

Glen Powell had nothing on Irish, but he sure was good to look at.

Where Glen Powell had dirty blonde hair, Irish's was a deep brown.

Almost the color of dark chocolate, and it was so soft.

He kept the sides trimmed down to a two, but on top, it was long and thick.

He had grey eyes. But his grey eyes were so unique in that they had little bursts of lilac in them.

They were undoubtedly my favorite feature of that man.

He was tall, too. Standing at six foot one, I loved it every time I stood beside him because he towered over me.

He was lean in some places but not in his arms or his thighs.

At just the mention of those powerful thighs and what he could do with them, my pussy clenched.

I shook my head and got back to work on Marjorie's hair.

Two hours later, I was walking into the clubhouse when I was snagged around the waist.

My body started to tense up until I caught the scent of the man.

And then I smiled, and my body relaxed.

"Good day?" He asked.

I nodded.

He lifted a brow at the bag I held, "What you got?"

I smiled and said slowly, "Imperial."

He groaned, "Please tell me you got enough for me too?"

I lifted a brow, "Why on earth would I do that for?"

"Because you always get me something when you go to Imperial, and it's our Tuesday date night. What movie are we watching?"

I giggled, all the while shaking my head.

Yes, I did get him food from Imperial.

The one time I forgot, he jumped on his bike in a torrential downpour and went and got his own.

But he almost didn't make it back due to a car hydroplaning right in front of him.

The memory of that night forever cemented itself in my mind.

I smiled up at him and said, "After what happened the one time, I forgot. Do you honestly think I would forget again?"

"If it were someone else... then yeah. But since it's you, then no." He said as he tapped the tip of my nose.

And just like that, we walked to my room in the clubhouse.

"Go get comfortable. I'll get what we need." He told me as he took the bag of food from my hand and set it on the small desk I had in there.

After I pulled on a tank and pajama bottoms, I took the elastic from my hair and shook it loose.

Then, I wiped off my makeup and moisturized.

When I returned to my room, I saw that Irish had everything laid out on the top of my bed, his kutte was hanging on the back of my door, and his boots were off as well.

Once I got settled, we started to eat. He asked, "Can I ask you something?"

I had just taken a bite of my dumpling, swallowed, and then nodded, "Yeah, you know you can ask me just about anything."

He smirked, fucker. "When you told us your story, why did you always full name that man? It's something I've been wanting to know, but I didn't want to put you in a bad place."

I sighed, "Because if I didn't, then he would beat me with a belt. But he only did it on parts of my body that my mother wouldn't see. And I know what you're thinking: why wouldn't I tell my mother what was going on?"

He nodded.

I sighed, then ran a hand through my hair, "Because if I ever told my mother what he was doing, he would carry out the threat to brand her with his name on her lower back. And he had a branding iron in his study. He showed it to me."

"I can't wait until I find that son of a bitch," he grumbled so low that I almost hadn't heard him.

But I had.

I lifted my brow, "Why are you trying to find him?"

"Because no one hurts you and gets away with it, Sutton. I already took care of Gerard. That fuckwad. And that motherfucker who wanted you for a wife. Now, all that's left is that son of a bitch."

At his words, I sat my container down and said, "Okay, I'm going to need you to break that statement down for me."

Because I was close to hyperventilating.

If I understood him right, he's already killed two men for me.

Me.

Holy. Shit.

He followed suit and sat his container down as well, locked his eyes with mine, and said, "Gerard was a piece of shit. He fucking pissed himself. The motherfucker who wanted you for a wife? He didn't. In fact, he was already married. He wanted a mistress, and when he was tired of you, he was going to give you to his men to do with as they pleased. I couldn't let a piece of trash like that keep on breathing."

I was frozen on the bed, but I had one thought, and only one, "Will you get in trouble for telling me any of that?"

He shook his head, "Nah. It wasn't club business, it was personal."

I nodded, then ignoring the containers, I vaulted over them and pressed my lips to his.

His hand came to the back of my head, tangled itself in my hair, and took over the kiss.

His tongue swept inside my mouth, and I moaned at the taste of him. Spice. Irish. Everything oh so nice.

When our kiss slowed, he pulled his lips from mine and whispered, "That's the payment I get for taking out a piece of shit, sign me the fuck up."

I laughed, then got back in my spot and was thankful to see that none of the containers had spilled.

We ate in silence. Just like we always did. Because when you are comfortable with someone, no words are needed.

We had just opened our second container when there was a knock at my door. Irish looked at me and asked, "You expecting someone?"

I shook my head.

He nodded, placed the remote down on the bed, got up, and went to the door.

He opened it a crack, and then when he saw who it was, he opened it the rest of the way.

Adeline stood in the doorway, taking everything in, and then I chuckled as she slapped her hand on her forehead, "Crap, today's Tuesday. Sorry. I forgot."

I giggled, "It's okay. What's up?"

She winced, "Well, I was going to see if you would ride with me somewhere. See, there's this kid in my class going through radiation. I've heard other kids making fun of her. Precious thing is losing her hair, and a chunk of it fell out while she was doing her classwork. Her mother can't afford to get her hair cut right now; she gets paid at the end of next week."

I smiled, then looked at Irish, "Imperial seems to always be better once you reheat it."

He chuckled, started putting the rest of the containers back in the bag, and then looked at me, "Get whatever you need, I'll meet you out front."

I nodded, then got out of bed, shucked off my tank and pajama bottoms, and pulled on a pair of leggings and a slouchy sweater.

Then I grabbed my kit and headed out of my room, and just in time for Irish to threaten, "There's a bag of food in the kitchen. Anyone fucks with it, and you'll get the beatdown of your fucking life."

I chuckled, then headed out front.

Adeline was standing beside Coal's bike.

Irish came out then, tagged my kit and my hand, and led me to his bike.

We were on the road in just a few minutes us, following Coal and Adeline.

Irish took a turn a little faster than he should have, and I giggled.

His hand came down to rub over the back of my leg. Oh, this man.

Fifteen minutes later, we were pulling into an area that wasn't the greatest in Fulton, Mississippi.

But with Irish and Coal, I knew that we didn't have anything to worry about.

I climbed off the bike in front of a faded mint green single-wide trailer.

Once the bikes were cut off, the screen door opened, and a woman stood there, she was visibly shaking.

Oh, man.

Adeline smiled at her, "Hi, Ms. Combs, I'm Mrs. Adams, Paisley's teacher. I called you before we came."

Ms. Combs seemed to soften at that, and gone was the shaking.

Once we reached the cement steps, she smiled, "Please, call me Holly, and come in."

A little girl was curled up under blankets on the couch in the living room. Dull eyes stared up at us.

Adeline moved first, kneeling in front of Paisley.

"Hey, Paisley. How are you feeling?" she asked her.

The little girl shrugged.

I let go of Irish's hand, not realizing it was wrapped in his, and followed suit with Adeline.

"Hi, Paisley, my name is Sutton. It's an honor to meet you."

She smiled, but it was missing the spark that most little kids always seemed to have.

"So, Mrs. Adams told me that some little mean kids made fun of you, I am so sorry about that. But... It's a good thing because I get to meet an amazing little fighter." I told her.

She smiled; a little spark came through.

I would take that.

"And you want to know something else? See the two big men behind me?" I asked her as I turned my head and looked back at Irish and Coal, then back at Paisley.

She nodded.

"I have a feeling that once we leave here tonight, they are going to pay a visit to all those mean kids and give them a good talking to. That alright with you?" I asked.

She giggled, then nodded.

Therefore, I continued, "I've been a hairdresser for almost two years now. I'm here to make that beautiful soul you have shine even brighter. I know this is going to be hard, but can I let you in on a little secret?"

Her eyes widened, and then she slowly nodded, "I've cut grown men's hair before, and they have bawled like a baby." I held up two fingers, "Girl code. We don't lie to other girls."

She giggled, then looked at her mother, and then back at me, and slowly nodded.

Once everything was set up, she was in a chair in the living room, both of her hands held by Adeline and her mother. I worked on cutting off all of her hair.

My heart broke for the little girl, and tears threatened to spill over my eyes. To hide how I was feeling, I knelt once I was finished and smiled up at her, then I whispered, "You know the good thing about having a bald head?"

She shook her head.

"You don't have to shampoo or condition. Makes bath time so much easier and gives you more time to play. But in your case, to make works of art. My girl, Mrs. Adams, told me about all the beautiful things you create."

With the back of her hand, she wiped at the tears on her cheek. Then I heard one of the sweetest voices I'd ever heard, "Would you like to see them?"

I smiled. If this little girl wanted to show me her art collection, then I would happily sit on my ass and marvel at each piece.

"You bet your cute little bootie I do," I told her.

She smiled, jumped out of the chair, and ran to another part of the house.

Her mother was wiping tears from her eyes when she whispered, "You didn't have to come. Thank you. She has a lot, if you need to leave, I'll understand."

I winked at her, "I gave her my word. I won't go back on it. She can have a million pieces of artwork, and I'll look at every single one of them. If that's alright with you."

The entire time, I felt eyes on me, and when I looked over my shoulder at Irish, it was to see nothing but pride in his gaze.

Oh, Irish, why?

Why can't you see what's right in front of you?

Just as I thought that, Paisley came back into the living room, plopped on the couch, and then proceeded to show me all of her artwork.

And it was artwork.

Some of it I could make out, some of it I couldn't, but I didn't let it show that I couldn't.

As I came across one picture, my breath caught. It was of a woman holding a child's hand with a rainbow in the background.

I looked at Paisley and asked, "Is this one spoken for?"

She scrunched her nose up, "What do you mean?"

I titled my head at it, "Well, most artists sell their work. So, have you already sold this one?"

She giggled, then shook her head, "No, I'm only seven."

I gasped, "You're only seven? With talent like this? I've just met a masterful artist. Dang, girl."

She giggled, then laughed.

Thankfully, I had some cash in my kit. I pulled it close and pulled the cash out and found a twenty and a ten, then I looked at Paisley and asked, "Would you take thirty dollars for this masterpiece?"

Her eyes went wide, her mouth fell open, and I couldn't contain my chuckle.

She looked from her mom, then to me, then back to her mom, and asked, "Mommy?"

"Your first paying customer. You had your eye on that new doll. That'll do it." Her mom barely got the last word out when Paisley looked at me and said, "Sold."

I grinned, then handed her the cash and said, "You have to sign it first. I want everyone to know who made this."

She grinned, then signed her first name at the bottom corner of the page.

Then something happened. Shocked the shit out of me to be frank.

Irish moved in, then dropped to his haunches and asked, "Let me look through your artwork, too. I need something to brighten up the space above my toolbox."

And that was how Irish had a one-of-a-kind drawing of a tree with a swing set hanging from it.

And that was also how Coal and Adeline both purchased artwork from Paisley.

Once I hugged Paisley and thanked her, I looked at Holly, "I work at Shear Salon, any time she needs something done with her hair or even your hair, y'all just call in and make an appointment with me, okay?"

She shook her head, "We can't afford it."

I smiled at her, "You're already affording it. That little girl already knows how much she's loved. There's not enough of that. And for the price of love, there's nothing I wouldn't do to make that person's life easier."

I tilted my head, "Tell you what, since my space at the salon looks a little drabby. My payment will be a new piece of never-before-seen artwork."

She gaped, "Are you serious?"

"Totally," I told her as I poured truth into that one word.

Twenty minutes later, in my bedroom, I curled into Irish and let the tears fall, "Explain to me how in the world within months, they had a shot for something they've never seen before, but they haven't been able to cure cancer in children yet."

He ran his hand through my hair, "I don't know, baby."

I asked, "Will you tell Coal and Adeline thank you for me?"

He nodded, not having to ask what I was asking him for.

He asked, "Ready to eat and watch the movie?"

I sighed, then shook my head, "No, I've lost my appetite."

"Alright. Get some sleep. You had a hard time with that. I'll stay until you fall asleep." He told me.

It was on the tip of my tongue to ask him to stay.

But the one time I did it, I got a firm and resounding no.

Rejection hurts, so I haven't asked him again.

Chapter 3
Irish

The prospects had just unloaded the last of the kegs for the party we had planned to celebrate Halloween,

Thankfully, we were having weather like we should be.

Which meant the high today was eighty-one degrees and the lowest today was fifty-four.

That meant it was the perfect weather for a barbeque, Mississippi-style.

And that also meant that just about everything would have comeback sauce in it. I rubbed my hands together. I couldn't wait.

The women were in the kitchen getting the side dishes ready while Whit prepared the grill. The man was a master at it.

How he got different meat to taste different with the coals and things he used, I would never know.

But when the meat hit your tongue, it was almost as good as an orgasm. Almost.

I was helping with placing the tree limbs and things into the area we had designated for the bonfire when the door opened, and the women started to file out with dishes in their hands.

I watched as Pipe dropped his log, then stormed over to Gabby, taking the dishes from her hands, Coal was growling at Adeline as he did the same.

I shook my head at the two of them, they were so pussy whipped it wasn't even fucking funny, but then... fucking Pagan, that motherfucker was there, taking the dishes that Sutton carried.

And when she gifted him with one of her smiles, I felt my fist clench, my jaw hardened.

Why the fuck hadn't I moved to help instead of criticizing Pipe and Coal.

Just as I was thinking that Stoney stepped to my side, "You're going to piss a ring around her tonight, brother. We all know it. But you won't move to help her. You can't get pissed off at Pagan. He's doing what any of us would do." And with that, he walked away.

The rumble of bikes arriving had all the brothers stopping what they were doing and making our way to the front of the clubhouse.

The Soulless Outlaws had arrived, as well as Pagan's Soldier's, Immoral Saints, and the closest Wrath MC charter to us, the one in Alabama, Willow's Crossing.

Asher shook hands with the Presidents. You had Nuke, Soulless Outlaws MC. Tomb, Pagan's Soldier's MC. Snake, Immoral Saint's MC. Declan, Wrath MC, Alabama chapter.

I greeted the road captains, Jury, Cali, Grenade, and Rocket.

I watched as Whit greeted his fellow Vice Presidents, Grey, Atlas, Vulcan, and Cross.

Trigger greeted his fellow treasurers, Xander, Coins, Scythe, and Tinker.

Pipe greeted his fellow secretaries, Jasper, Eagle, Magnum, and Bash.

Coal moved to jerk his chin at his fellow icers, Grimm, Koffin, Tyne, and Rhage.

Priest shook the hands of his fellow enforcers, Kettle, Slater, Slayer, and Havoc.

Rome moved to greet his fellow sergeant at arms, Khal, Kodiak, Phantom, and Thrash.

Stoney met everyone, the blunt old fucker.

Four vans followed the bikes as women and club hangers on's climbed out of them, fixing their mini-skirts and fluffing their hair. I caught sight of Cynnamin's blonde hair.

Adeline moved to Coal's side.

Gabby moved to Pipes.

Stella moved to Asher's while dragging Chloe, her best friend and the one woman who had Asher's undivided attention, she just didn't know it. And neither did Stella. Yet.

Sutton was there walking through the men, and then she stepped to my side.

Nothing could have made me puff my chest out more.

But I didn't like the looks she was getting.

She wasn't claimed.

And after what she had been through, she didn't need to be claimed. It would be her decision.

And god help the lucky motherfucker that got to call that woman his.

It wouldn't be me, though.

What woman wanted a man that no one wanted?

Not even his parents.

Why else would they have dropped him off outside a fire station when he was only four years old? And then bounced around from foster home to foster home. Each home ended up getting worse and worse.

And all that any of them wanted was to collect a fucking paycheck.

I felt a hand rest on my forearm, looking down into Sutton's eyes, she lifted a brow, then mouthed, "Are you okay?" she asked as she squeezed.

I jerked my chin at her, then pulled my arm from her grip and went back to work on creating the bonfire.

After I got some whiskey in my system, my earlier words faded, and like whiskey always did, it heightened my sex drive.

The party was raging at full force, and when I saw Sutton bend to a cooler and tag one of those sweet teas she loved, my dick got hard.

Jesus Christ, but she had the perfect ass.

Each globe fit deliciously in my hand.

Sadly, when she did that, it got more than one pair of eyes on her. Hands moved to adjust their junk, but they wouldn't be in her bed, no, I would be there.

Or... yeah, correct that, she would be in my bed.

No way in fucking hell was I going to leave her bed only for some motherfucker to knock on her door later in the night.

Which was why I walked over to her. From the corner of her eye, she must have seen me coming, she smiled. I said, "You're in my bed tonight. Alright?"

She nodded, then smiled that full-blown smile of hers.

And damn, but I would do anything to receive those full-blown smiles of hers.

***

The women had knocked the food out of the fucking park.

I was so full that I doubted an hour would be enough time for the food to settle.

Nevertheless, everyone was looking forward to tonight.

A lot of dick measuring was going to be taking place.

And then a conversation I had overheard from the women made me chuckle; it had gone like this.

Lizette, "I want a man with a big sausage, stretch me so wide, I can't breathe."

Gabby, "Umm, yeah, no, I like my vagina the way it is. I don't need it ripping."

Adeline, "I've only ever seen one, and it's perfect."

Sutton, "I don't think size matters. Those books I read, as long as a man knows how to work his cock, then size doesn't matter."

She was right. So fucking right.

I was taken from my thoughts when Asher climbed into the ring, brought two fingers to his lips, and whistled.

Since all the food was consumed, everyone had time to let their food settle because no one wanted to get puked on by someone who had been punched in the gut.

"We are honored to host this event. The changing of the seasons. And in honor of the changing seasons, it's time for some retribution. If you want to claim your manhood back, sign up. If you have a dispute to settle, sign up. If you want to claim a woman for the night, sign up. And if you just want to beat someone's ass, then sign the fuck up."

Every man moved to where Pipe was sitting at a table with Gabby at his side.

Once I signed my name, I crossed my arms over my chest and waited.

Pipe was done and came to stand with me, followed by Coal.

Asher moved over with Whitt, Trigger, Priest, and Stoney.

Rome moved then, too.

"I'm so getting fucked good tonight." I heard Gabby say.

Lizette, "Right. Last time this happened, Trigger was relentless."

"I learned that public sex is the best kind of sex," Adeline chimed in.

The girls looked at her and then busted out laughing.

"What about you, Sutton, who are you waiting for to take you all night long?" Lizette asked her.

"Already been claimed for the night. And I can't wait." She said with a huskiness in her tone.

At her tone and the way she said it, I shifted my legs to get my dick in a better place. I was looking forward to it, too.

The rounds had begun.

Phantom did some kind of ninja shit and knocked Rocket on his ass.

Koffin threw one punch and knocked Beast the fuck out.

It was a draw between Slayer and Slater.

It was Stoney's turn.

Dawg, the tech man for Pagan's Soldiers, stepped into the ring.

That was when Dawg pointed into the crowd.

I looked through everyone, and when I saw who he was pointing at, I felt my jaw clench.

I don't think so motherfucker.

I could feel my brother's eyes on me. Priest lowered his tone, "Brother, you gotta let it play out. You do it, shows you claimed her."

Whitt spoke next, "We all see it. Even if you don't. But brother, make a move or get off the pot."

Did they see the same thing I did?

If they had, they wouldn't be telling me the shit they were.

One, Dawg had earned his name. He was a fucking player.

Two, he was around the same age as her stepfather... the same man that ordered her to be raped.

And three... fuck it, I didn't need another reason.

I didn't hesitate to climb into the ring and tap Stoney on the shoulder.

He looked over at me, smirked, then climbed out of the ring.

Dawg looked at me, read my road name, and taunted, "Funny, you don't look like an Irishman."

I smirked, "Nah. But they see why I'm called that once they've pissed me off. And that's something you're about to find out about."

Without waiting a single second, I threw a punch into the side of his head, just right, and I smirked as he went down like a sack of bricks.

Then I popped my neck, looked at Pipe, and said, "Who's up next?"

A few of the brothers from the Pagans moved into the ring to drag Dawg's body out of the ring.

Then, the man I was slated to fight climbed into the ring.

Oh, this was going to be fun.

Jury smirked at me and then asked, "You ready, brother?"

I winked, "Bring it."

We moved at the same time.

***

My hand was fisted in Sutton's hair as I pounded into her from behind, my free hand went to her clit where I thrummed it with my thumb.

When she let out a moan, I asked, "You like that, baby?"

She moaned, "Yes, do that again. Fuck me, Irish, please."

Her wish was my command.

I rotated my hips and slammed into her over and over and over.

Only then did I feel her pussy clench around my cock did I let myself go into the condom.

I stilled.

Feeling the orgasm shoot out of my cock and into her heat.

Then I had the sudden thought to forgo a condom... Jury hadn't landed a single hit to my head... where the fuck did that thought come from?

I pulled out of her while shaking my head, tugging the condom off, tying it, and tossing it in the trash can.

When Sutton moved, somehow, she popped her body, and I got a view of that delectable pussy, fuck it.

I had my arm at her waist, lifting her body while walking us toward the wall.

Her legs went to the tops of my shoulders, her hands went to my hair, her nails digging into my scalp as I feasted on her pussy.

I swirled my tongue around her clit, as my hands squeezed her ass.

Just as I flicked her clit in random succession, she moaned, "Irish, fuck."

I grinned into her pussy and repeated it, and I knew that if she hadn't cared, the locks of my hair would have been pulled out with how hard she was gripping it now.

"Irish, I'm about to come," I thought about telling her to let go, to give me all of it, but then I thought better of it.

I growled, "Not without me."

And then I pulled my mouth from her pussy, lowered her body, pressed my mouth to hers, and in one swift move, I slammed my cock into her hot heat. And. I. Froze.

Holy. Fuck.

The way her pussy felt wrapped around my cock, my only thought was that I had died and gone to heaven.

Her pussy was so warm, sheathing my cock.

And I swear to Christ, it got even harder than it ever had before.

I gritted through my teeth, "Are you on birth control?"

She nodded, "Yeah, when I became a club girl officially, I had them install the implant. It's good for another..." She didn't finish.

Because of her words, I pulled out and slammed back in.

Groaning.

Moaning.

Gritting my teeth so hard it would be a wonder if I didn't have a locked jaw after this.

I was pounding into her so hard now that slaps against my door could be heard.

But I didn't slow, and Sutton paid them no mind.

Especially when she screamed, "Irish. Fuck. Yes. Do that again."

I did it again.

And again.

And again.

It felt so good that I didn't want this to end, but when I moved my hips just right, her pussy clamped down on my cock, and that was all I felt.

That was all my dick needed to feel.

Because her warm essence flowed around my cock, and I was shooting off inside of her.

We were both breathing heavily, trying to draw air into our lungs.

My arms were shaking from where I was holding her up, and my knees were shaking.

But even through all of that, I still carefully lowered her to her feet.

She didn't move once her feet were solidly underneath her.

I smirked, "You alright?"

She nodded, then smiled, "Yeah, umm, can we do that again, but on a bed this time?"

I winked, "Give me five."

And then, I repeated the moves on her body well throughout the night.

There wasn't a place on her body my hands and mouth didn't touch.

But Sutton wasn't the type of woman to do all the work.

Oh no. After we had caught our breath, she then proceeded to kiss the bruises that had already formed on my body, moving down until she reached my cock.

And when she wrapped her lips around the head, I closed my eyes and knew I wouldn't hesitate to kill again for this woman.

***

I wasn't sure how early it was, but I was still wired and could go another round. But I allowed Sutton to do something I've yet to let anyone do.

Fall asleep in my bed.

But it wasn't the sex we'd had all fucking night long that had me wired.

No... it was the whispered words I heard just as she fell into a cat nap.

"I love you, Irish."

Fuck. Me.

Chapter 4
Sutton

I pressed my hands to my cheeks, hoping that they weren't flaming red after the positions Irish had put me in well into the early morning hours.

Dawn was kissing the sky as I walked down the steps from his room and headed into the kitchen to help with breakfast.

But first, I needed substance. Therefore, I headed to the fridge, not making eye contact with the women already in the room.

Tagging the tub of vanilla yogurt, I then headed to the pantry and grabbed the granola.

Just as I turned to set my things on the island, I heard someone snort, "You get branded last night?"

Yep, I was sure that if my cheeks hadn't been flaming earlier, they were now.

And I knew exactly what she was referring to. Damn Gabby.

Sighing, I tagged my bowl and settled onto a bar stool.

Just then, Irish walked into the kitchen, tagging the last plate with the last omelet on it.

I watched him walk to a table, sit, and chow down.

But him not looking at me as he entered had my heart hurting. Damn, but how many times was he going to do this?

To hide my hurt and the direction my thoughts were going, I tried to ignore him as I ate my yogurt and granola.

It wasn't until he shifted in his seat that I realized how I, too, had shifted on my bar stool so I could keep him in my sights.

I watched as he apparently finished his omelet, stood, and then brought the plate to Gabby, winked at her, and then walked out, all the while ignoring me.

My shoulders dropped; I couldn't help it.

What more did I need to do to show that man how I felt about him?

My eyes went to Gabby as she grabbed a hand towel to dry her hands after she cleaned up Irish's mess, and then she lowered her voice and said, "Honey, as far as I know, he hasn't slept with any of the other club girls."

I inhaled a breath as I tried to keep the tears at bay, but when one of them rolled down from the corner of my eye, I didn't even try to catch it and smiled, but I knew it was weak. "I know. Pres is getting pretty pissed off at him, I do know that. He claims I'm his, but he won't do anything about it either. He warns all the brothers that try to come onto me, too."

Gabby nodded, then asked, "He doesn't want you but doesn't want anyone else to have you?"

I nodded solemnly. "Maybe it's time to move on. We've been doing this dance for a year and a half now."

"You going to try to be with one of the other brothers tonight?" She asked.

"I'm thinking about it. But I just… I don't want whoever it is to get hurt. You saw what happened the last time a brother from another chapter grabbed me around the waist while we were dancing." I shuttered after remembering in grave detail what had happened.

The guy that I had been dancing with had wrapped his hand around my back to pull me in closer, something so simple.

But where his hand had landed? It was right at the top of my ass. It really was nothing, but it wasn't too Irish.

He had stormed over there, grabbed the man's hand, and wrenched his arm back too far. We all heard a pop when he dislocated the guy's shoulder.

As if that wasn't enough, Irish had grabbed me, pulled me behind him, and then, while he still held onto the guy's arm, he maneuvered him to the ground roughly then, with one of his steel-toe boots, he slammed it down hard into his side.

And that was how that other guy suffered four broken ribs, a punctured lung, and a dislocated shoulder, not to mention torn tendons.

I shook my head at the memory and heard Gabby say, "You can always talk to Asher."

"I could, but after what happened with Hallie this morning, I don't want to stir up any more drama."

Because Hallie had broken one of the bigger rules that we club girls had.

She had been poking condoms with needles in hopes of getting knocked up by Whit.

Needless to say, once it was discovered, which was earlier this morning, while Irish and I poked our heads out of his room, we didn't need any more drama.

But just as I thought that, I heard the door to the clubhouse open, and from where I was sitting, I only had to tilt my head to see who it was.

And when I saw one of the men, I sighed.

Because it meant that she was here.

The woman I wanted to murder.

The woman who I knew Irish was also doing things with.

And it tore a piece of my heart every time I saw her face.

Then it tore a bigger piece every time I had to watch as Irish took her hand and led her up to his room.

And I would have to endure all of that for the rest of the day and well into the night.

Because the Soulless Outlaws were staying here for the weekend, Pagan's Soldier's MC, Immoral Saints MC, and Wrath MC had pulled out before breakfast had started.

I was thankful I hadn't seen her last night.

That would have ruined everything.

Just like it did right now.

The euphoria I was feeling after last night and the fact that I had woken up to him after a few hours of sleep.... had faded. Completely.

Kill me now.

Thankfully, Gabby said, "I have to watch the kids tonight, and knowing Stella, she will shoo me out of the room so I can enjoy the party. I'll run interference if you want me to."

I sighed in gratefulness, "You're awesome, girl. I think that would be great."

Throughout the day, I helped with lunch for everyone, hung out with the girls, talked to a few of the guys, and not once did Irish speak to me.

And he hadn't gone near Cynnamin either.

So, what the hell was going on with him?

I was about to ask him what was going on when a song blasted through the speakers. And I smiled.

I looked for Rome, and when my eyes landed on him, I headed in his direction and tilted my head to the side.

Rome jerked his chin to the chair at his side.

Once I was settled in, he pulled out a notebook, and for the remainder of the song, we played Hangman.

When I was brought into the clubhouse the very first time, I didn't know what was going on or what was happening.

They'd worked on calming me down and getting my story, and I got it, I did.

They had an unknown in their midst, and they needed to know things.

When everyone went to a room they called church, I brought my knees to my chest and hugged them.

But Rome being Rome, he didn't go into the room, no, he sat down beside me, pulled out a little notebook, and proceeded to play hangman with me. All while this same song played in the background.

I was laughing before I could stop myself at the words he was using.

And just like then, as he was doing now, the words cocksucker, twat waffle, and my favorite, goat licker, filled his pages.

I was still laughing when I saw it.

My body tensed.

Rome's eyes followed the direction I was looking in, and from the corner of my eye, I saw that his jaw hardened.

I sat there, visibly shaken, as he did it.

I had been waiting all day for it to happen.

Hoping beyond hope that since he didn't do anything with her yesterday, that just maybe...

I had been trying to shore up my defenses to deafen the hurt I was about to endure.

But every time I tried that method, it only made it hurt even worse.

The last thing I saw was Irish grabbing her ass and leading her into the clubhouse.

After everything last night.

After knocking that guy out because he pointed at me and basically tried to claim me for the night...

I couldn't keep doing this.

It was breaking my heart piece by freaking piece.

I knew I couldn't not give myself to one of the brothers.

I knew that.

But I would be damned if I gave myself to Irish again.

Fuck.

That.

He had lost that right.

.... only one more month and seventeen days, and I would be fulfilling my contract with the club.

If Irish hadn't changed his tune by then, well, I would be leaving.

I couldn't handle any more of this hurt.

Just then, a shadow fell over me.

Lifting my gaze, it was to see Pagan.

One of the new prospects who had been given his patch, therefore, I smiled up at him, "Looks good on you."

He winked down at me, then lowered to his haunches, "Want to get out of here for a bit? Too many fucking people that I don't know."

I smiled, then said what the hell.

I nodded, then he stood, offered me his hand, and helped me up.

His hand went to the small of my back and led me out of the courtyard, around the clubhouse, and to his bike.

He tagged his helmet and handed it to me while saying, "Know you love Irish. It's written plain as fuck on your face, sweetheart. And as much as I would love the opportunity to show your body the pleasures I can give it, I won't. Because I will be damned to have the woman I'm fucking, thinking about someone else. So, this is just a ride. Any time you need it. Okay?"

I smiled, then took the helmet he offered to me, "Anytime you need to be reminded, you're a good man, Pagan. You just come to me, and I'll set you straight."

And with that, I climbed onto his bike after he did.

Then he started the engine, and we were off.

Taking the backroads and letting the pleasure of being on the back of the bike ebb away some of the hurt.

Chapter 5
Irish

Once I finished with Cynnamin, I winked at her and said, "Thanks. It's always a fun time with you."

She winked, "Why do you think I always come here? You give it so good, Irish."

I winked back at her and then headed down the stairs and out to the courtyard, with Cynnamin trailing me until we walked past a set of tables.

I was straightening my clothes, my eyes scanning the courtyard for Sutton to make sure some little punk ass wasn't messing with her.

I frowned then when I didn't get a sight of her ashy brown hair that I liked a whole hell of a lot.

I did another scan and then locked eyes on Gabby from where she was sitting beside Pipe.

Knowing Gabby would know where Sutton was because the two of them were as tight as two women could be.

The moment I reached Gabby, I asked, "You seen Sutton?"

She nodded, took a sip from her beer, and said, in a weird way, as if she didn't care, "I saw Pagan take her into the clubhouse." Then she looked at her watch, "That was hours ago. You need her?"

I took in a breath.

Fucking. Hell.

Fucking Pagan?

I was still learning about him, but I knew that he didn't deserve to be in the same breathable space as Sutton when I took in a breath and let it out, then asked, "What did he need her help with?"

She simply shrugged. "Not sure, but well, she liked whatever he said to her. She jumped out of her chair lightning quick."

I felt it, why I was called Irish. My temper was riled. I knew my neck had just flushed scarlet red as my nostrils flared, "You mean?"

Gabby sat her beer on the table, then leaned on her forearms, "You know me, Irish, you know I'm blunt and tell it like it is, so I don't want to hear a single word for disrespecting you for what I have to say. Everyone knows how she feels about you. Everyone also knows how you act whenever another brother even talks to Sutton. We also know that whenever that other woman comes here, you drop Sutton like a hot potato. It's not fair to Sutton. Make a choice. Because it happens again, you won't just have a pissed-off Sutton to deal with."

Just as I opened my mouth to say something, like it was between me and Sutton, and when I realized I needed to talk to Cynnamin to see if she was okay with me talking to Sutton, I saw Pagan and Sutton walking back into the courtyard.

And something about the way Sutton looked caused my gut to tighten.

She was glowing.

But I felt a smirk tug at my lips because I had seen her truly glow, and the look she was sporting now wasn't the same.

Not like when I finished pounding my cock into her tight heat with her hands tied behind her back.

But then I stood there as I watched Pagan lean down and whisper something in her ear, and she blushed, my temper was fraying, which caused me to bellow, "The fuck did you do?"

I watched as Pagan stood his ground, crossed his arms over his chest, and shot me a glare.

You little motherfucker.

And before I could say anything more, it was Sutton who spoke and caused my temper to slowly come back under control, but then... well... it flared up again.

"Went for a ride. I'm surprised you're done with your whore already. Normally, you spend the night with her in your bed. Hope she realizes how special she is. Cause even I don't get that."

And with that, Sutton shoulder-checked me and then started to walk away.

But my dumbass self spoke when I shouldn't have.

And my temper got the best of me.

"So, what, my dick wasn't good enough for you now? You whore." I shouldn't have said that. Not to her. Fuck. Me.

Sutton stopped in her tracks and turned stiffly towards me, and I tried to hide the feeling that I knew I just fucked up with her, but something told me it was too late.

And I knew it was when she said, "Last time I checked, ever since I joined the MC, it's only been your dick that's been in my mouth and my pussy. But my body sure as hell hasn't been the only place your dick has been. But, after that bike ride with Pagan, he wants to fuck me seven ways to Sunday? I just might let him. Oh, and the last time I checked, I know I've been with one man willingly my whole life, and that's you. I bet your whore can't say the same, and neither can you. So, watch who the hell you call a whore. And if you ever call me one again after what I went through almost two years ago, I'll kill you."

You could've heard a pin drop as Sutton stormed to the side of the clubhouse and left.

I didn't see my brothers get up and close in on me.

But I sure as hell felt the punch Rome slammed into my face.

He lowered his tone dangerously and said, "We all know what that girl went through. She was raped. And you have the nerve to call her a whore. The only reason none of us have even tried to be with her was that you were the only one she trusted."

I stood still because I fucking deserved everything they were about to dish out.

Even the punch from Coal to my kidney.

Also, the punch from Pipe to my other kidney.

By the time they were finished, I turned stiffly and headed into the clubhouse.

A plan was formulated in my mind on how I could get Sutton to forgive me.

But first, I needed to down some painkillers.

Once I did that, I made my way, not to my room or anyone else, but to the hallway the club girls used.

And then I sat down as carefully as I could and leaned my head back against the wall outside her bedroom.

What. The. Fuck. Was. I. Doing.

I heard Sutton whisper those three little words to me.

So why the fuck was I holding onto the pride of not telling her what was really going on with me and Cynnamin and setting her ass straight?

Then I repeated those same words in my head, "A man isn't a man at all if he doesn't keep his word."

Fuck.

Just then, my phone rang.

I pulled it out, and at the same time, Sutton opened her door.

When she saw me sitting there, she narrowed her eyes and slammed the door closed.

Fucking. Hell.

I looked at who was calling and felt my brows raise.

Why the hell was he calling me?

Answering the call, I asked, "Declan, what's going on?"

"You plotted out that trip through the Louisiana Bayou and avoided the game wardens. Think you can do that again for me?"

"I can, but I gotta have all the info. You cool with that?" I asked him.

"Yeah, when can you make the ride?" he asked.

My eyes went toward Sutton's door and the way she saw me sitting there and closed the door.

"I'll ride out once I speak to Asher." Once we hung up, I called Asher, and he answered on the third ring.

I rode out half an hour later and headed to Alabama.

With Trigger at my side.

Not knowing that a storm was brewing and I would need my anchor to keep me steady.

Chapter 6
Irish

It was four days later, our bikes were eating up the open road headed for home when my phone rang, and thankfully, I had a Bluetooth helmet, answering the call, I said, "Yo?"

Asher's voice came through, and he asked, "Where are you?"

I thought about it and said, "About half an hour or so from the clubhouse, what's going on?"

"I don't care about any laws you break, get your ass here. Now." Then he hung up.

I nodded, then signaled to Trigger, and together we sped toward the clubhouse.

Making it there in fifteen minutes.

On the way there, I had no idea what was awaiting me.

My first thought was if anyone fucked with Sutton, I would be adding more souls to my calling card.

My second thought was someone had messed with Adeline, Gabby, Stella, or even Chloe.

But then I nixed all of those.

If someone had messed with any of those women, they wouldn't be calling me asking where I was.

No, they'd be handling the situation.

But of all the scenarios that went through my head, nothing could have prepared me for what was really waiting for me at the clubhouse.

Chapter 7
Sutton

I was still feeling murderous towards that man, and I couldn't calm down.

But what choice did I fucking have.

He wasn't mine.

Even though I wanted him to be.

I just wanted to be the only woman with him.

So what could I do?

I knew a little bit about Irish's past, but any time I'd pushed him on the subject, he had closed down on me.

And if reliving those memories would be hard for him, then I didn't need to know.

I didn't want him to hurt.

God, I was such a sucker for that man.

There he was, hurting me left and fucking right.

And here I was worrying about hurting him?

I needed to have my head examined, or at the very least, I needed to have someone operate and have my heart replaced with that of an uncaring and unfeeling bitch.

Perhaps switch mine with Cynnamin's.

Yeah, that would definitely work.

I still hadn't seen nor talked to Irish.

It's been four days since that night.

I know he left to go do something for the club.

I shook my head, enough of this shit.

I had a jam-packed day with clients, and I needed to finish getting ready.

I was excited for today.

I was going to be giving Paisley's mom a well-deserved makeover.

Just then, my phone rang, and when I saw it was Asher, I frowned.

I answered it just as I slipped my feet into my shoes, "Hello?"

"Sutton, I know you're pissed at Irish, but he needs you, honey."

I froze, "What's going on?"

"Come down to the front gate," And with that, Asher hung up.

I frowned down at my phone as I lowered it from my ear.

I hurried through getting ready and then grabbed my bags, and headed out of my room, down the hall, and to the front door.

Once I opened it, my eyes scanned the courtyard.

And then my breath caught in my lungs.

There was a little girl in a pink flowery dress that I had seen in my dreams.

The hair.

The eyes.

The nose.

The lips.

The mouth.

Everything that was Irish.

Everything I had dreamed our child would look like.

But another bike pulled into the courtyard.

The rider atop it was one I hadn't met before.

As I took in his kutte, I was able to make out the words *Creature* and *Nomad*. And he had on a Zagan MC kutte.

Almost as if I had conjured the man, he came roaring into the courtyard with Trigger hot on his heels.

My gaze shifted from him to the little girl, then back to Irish.

I watched as Asher walked over to him and said something.

Irish's gaze whipped to the little girl, and then I watched as his body tensed.

Then I stood there, just as everyone else did, and watched as Irish climbed off his bike and walked slowly to the little girl.

Her eyes were wide as she took everyone in.

For some reason, her gorgeous gray eyes stilled on me for a split second longer than anyone else, and then they moved to Irish and watched him as he made it to her.

I watched as Irish knelt in front of the little girl.

They spoke for long minutes.

Then she handed him a white envelope.

He took it, opened it, and pulled out what looked to be a sheet of paper.

And I watched him read whatever was on that piece of paper.

It seemed he was finished, then his head turned, he surveyed everyone, and when his eyes came to me, he jerked his chin.

Yes, I was pissed the hell off at him, but no way in hell would I take it out on that precious little girl.

I was in her spot once; yes, I was older, but still, I had an inkling as to what she was going through.

When I made my way over to them, I knelt, and then Irish handed me a letter.

I took in his face before I took the letter and saw that the paper was slightly crinkled where he had held onto it and clenched it. The anger I could see sitting just below the surface. What shocked me was that he hadn't already ripped the paper in half.

Taking it gingerly, I started to read,

'Dear Irish, I'm sure you don't remember me. Heck, I barely remember that night, but I know that I was with no one else a month before that night and a month after that night. Her name is Maisie April Smith. She was born on the seventh of December, two thousand and twenty. She weighed six pounds and nine ounces. My name is Kendra, by the way. I can't care for her like I should, I've gotten in a spot of trouble. So, I am giving her to you. All the necessary forms are in her bag. I'm not sure if you remember the event or not, we were both plenty drunk. I would have wanted a repeat... but no woman wants to hear the man that's currently inside of her say another woman's name.'

Once I finished reading it, I looked at Irish and handed him the letter, "First thing, we need to get her into the clubhouse. She's not dressed properly for this weather. Second thing, you need to find a house or an apartment. Third, I don't think you need it, but you need a DNA test done."

He looked at me, looking deeply into my eyes, and he whispered, "Will you help me?"

I took in a breath, looked at Maisie, then back at Irish, and nodded.

I smiled at Maisie, damn, but I loved that name, and said, "Hi, Maisie, my name is Sutton. What do you say about going inside where it's warm and finding some milk and cookies?" I asked her as I handed her my hand.

She looked at it, then at everyone, and I could see the fear in her gray gaze. Therefore, I lowered my voice, "My favorite cartoon character is Minnie Mouse. Do you know who that is?"

Her eyes widened, and then she nodded.

"I want you to picture all the men in Minnie Mouse ears, a pink bow, and a fluffy pink skirt on them," I told her, chuckling when she giggled.

And then... she placed her little hand in mine, and she didn't know it yet, but the pieces of my heart that Irish hadn't touched just became hers.

I stood then and led her inside, everyone following in our wake.

I looked at Gabby and asked, "Will you call the salon and send a text to my clients for me?"

Since she was the one to help me set up my calendar, she wouldn't have any issues in doing so. She nodded, then took my phone that I had offered to her.

We were in the kitchen, and I had just lifted Maisie and settled her onto the counter.

I got out the milk and the package of cookies when Irish walked in, followed by Asher and Charlie.

Irish looked at Maisie as I got everything poured into glasses and the package of cookies opened.

"Can you tell me when your mommy dropped you off?" Irish asked her.

She shrugged, "I know she woke me up with a smile. She doesn't do that a lot. Usually, she wakes me up by screaming at me."

That. Fucking. Bitch.

"Okay, do you know how long it took you to get here?" he asked.

She shook her head, "No. But she didn't want me to ever call her mommy. She had me call her Kendra."

I gritted my teeth.

That. Fucking. Bitch.

To hide what I was thinking and feeling, I took a cookie, dabbed it in the milk, and then handed it to her.

She smiled, then took the cookie.

While we waited for the lawyer to show up and someone to perform the DNA test, I asked Maisie, "What's your favorite meal?"

She smiled after taking another bite of cookie, "Mac N cheese."

I gasped, "No way! That's mine, too. What's your favorite candy?"

She looked befuddled, then asked, "What's that?"

I repeat. That. Fucking. Bitch.

I walked to the pantry, grabbed the candy dish that never seemed to get empty, and pulled out a Kit Kat bar.

I opened it and handed it to her, and then I took one for myself.

She took a bite, and then her eyes widened and smiled, then I laughed as she shoved the whole thing in her mouth.

A friend of the club came by and performed a DNA test, and since this was a timely manner, she put a rush on it.

The club's lawyer also came by, looked at the documentation, and nodded.

"I'll get this before the judge and let him know a DNA test has been performed. In the meantime, you need to get her everything she needs."

I nodded at him and then looked at Irish, "I need your credit card."

He opened his wallet and handed it to me.

Then I looked at Maisie, "Okay, sweet girl. What's your favorite color?"

She smiled and said, "Pink."

I winked at her and whispered, "Mine too."

I left her with Irish and the guys, and then me and the girls went to Target and got her everything she would need but bedding and furniture.

And since she seemed to cling to me, she was in my room at the clubhouse most of the time.

Then, four days later, the results revealed what was blatantly obvious.

Four days after that, myself, along with Gabby, Adeline, Lizette, Stella, and Chloe, bought everything that Irish would need for his house.

And we got things that would make any little girl happy.

Irish and I still haven't talked about things.

Between reworking my hours so I could be with Maisie and his club responsibilities on top of those at the garage, I ended up on the couch at his new house.

And it was stunning.

He was able to get one of the newly built houses with all the amenities they had to offer. It was a dark blue in color with light-washed accents. I loved it. I truly did.

If I had seen this house before he bought it, I would have championed it.

It had a nice front yard. And a backyard that was fenced in.

And yes, I know what you're thinking. Why would I agree to help Irish after everything... simple.

Because that little girl was neglected and thrown away as if she were nothing but trash.

And I wouldn't, no, I refused to treat her that same way.

Chapter 8
Irish

My phone had pinged earlier in the day, and it was Sutton asking if she could cook dinner for everyone.

I had agreed because, one, that sounded great.

And second, it would be good for Maisie.

Walking into my house, the first thing I saw was Sutton in one of my long old sleeve button-down shirts with a pair of my socks pulled all the way up to her knees.

The second thing I saw was my daughter at her side, wiggling her little booty to the song that they had blasting through my speakers. What was adorable was that my little girl was in one of mine, too, but the sleeves were rolled up, and the shirt was dancing with the floor.

They were both laughing and dancing, each holding one of her hair brushes as they belted out Sutton's favorite song.

The feel of my brothers at my back hit me as I stepped into the house and then just watched as the show played out.

Seeing as neither one of them heard me open the door, they were still dancing around.

My brothers picked up the song at my back and were singing right along with them.

Wanting to take part in this, I toed off my boots, and the moment Bob Segar said, "*Still like that old-time rock & roll*, I slid into the fray and started singing with them.

***

We pulled into the clubhouse after finding jack shit about Kendra.

It was almost as if she had faded off the face of the planet.

I checked my phone, wondering if Sutton had sent me a text or anything, but there was nothing.

Everyone gathered around Asher's bike, he ran his hand through his hair, "I gotta get home to Stella, so this is going to be short. Let Charlie see what he can find out. Irish, don't worry about any runs we need to make, all that's on hold. Your daughter is what's important. I'll see y'all tomorrow."

And like that, we separated.

I climbed back on my bike and headed towards my house.

And the whole way, I did nothing but think.

My fucking house.

Sure, I knew I wouldn't live in the clubhouse forever.

But I didn't know it was going to be this soon.

Yes, I had a lot of money in the bank, so buying the house wasn't the problem.

The problem was I didn't know the first thing about turning a house into a home.

But the first thought about the house I had was that Sutton would love it.

Why, why couldn't I make up my mind?

Almost every waking thought I'd had since I met Sutton had been about the woman.

I sighed as I climbed off my bike and walked to the front door.

Once I had it unlocked, I walked inside and closed the door.

And when I saw the pink boots sitting by the door, I had only one thought.

I was a father.

Holy. Fucking. Shit.

My gaze went right to the couch.

Sutton was right. She did look just like me.

Right down to the tips of her toes.

She was my mini-clone in every sense of the word.

My gray eyes, my dark brown hair, my nose, my fingers, my toes, my ears.

Jesus.

And as I stood there staring at the couch where Sutton and Maisie were curled up fast asleep, with some movie in the background playing on low... Had you told me last month that I would be here right now, I would have called you a liar.

I didn't know anything about kids.

Fucking nothing.

Plus, what did I know about caring for anything other than my bike and my club?

I wasn't shown what a home is supposed to be.

I wasn't told I love you.

Never heard the words directed at me until Sutton said them in her sleep.

And yeah, I'm still kicking my ass for acting like a little pussy ever since that night.

The two of us needed to talk.

I just didn't know how to start that conversation.

And when I laid out my feelings... well... what I thought were my feelings, I knew that Sutton would leave and wouldn't look back.

Now, it's hard to remember my life before Sutton came into it.

I heard a saying one time, *'The ones that come into your life and are meant to be there will leave a lasting impact on your life.'*

That was so true. It wasn't even funny how true it was.

But in the next instant, it was almost as if she could feel me in the house, her head lifted, her eyes opened, and they came to me.

And no, I didn't miss the way she pulled Maisie closer to her body as her eyes adjusted.

And when she saw that it was me, her grip loosened.

She mouthed, "Hey."

I jerked my chin.

Then I moved to the couch, carefully gathered Maisie in my arms, and carried her to her new bedroom that the women...mainly Sutton, had created a room that any princess would adore.

Right down to the white netting shit that was like a canopy over her bed.

Once I laid Maisie down and covered her up, I did something that felt natural. As natural as breathing.

I lowered my head and pressed a kiss on her temple.

She snuggled into the covers.

Carefully, I backed out of her room, went to the fridge, and tagged a beer for myself and a bottle of sweet tea for Sutton, then I looked at her.

She was pulling her shoes on, so I called out softly, "Wanna stay and have a drink with me?"

She looked at me, then at the beer in my hand and the sweet tea in my other one, then back at me, and nodded.

I led her to the front porch and settled into one of the white rocking chairs that Priest had dropped off.

We rocked in silence as we took sips from our bottles, and then I opened my mouth and said, "How the fuck do I do this?"

She was silent, and then she whispered, "You just do it. She's yours, Irish. And from what I can tell, she hasn't had the greatest life. What child doesn't know what candy is?"

"See, you're still pissed off about that," I told her.

She growled, "I don't see how anyone wouldn't be."

I nodded.

We were both silent. I was taking in her words, and she seemed to be gearing up to say something, and I didn't like that.

Normally, Sutton just said what was on her mind, rarely did she hesitate.

But I'd noticed that lately, she seemed to be hesitating with me.

And I didn't like it.

I know I caused it.

But I didn't fucking like it.

Her voice floated over the cold breeze when she said, "You just have to love her Irish. I know the concept is foreign to you, but that's all she needs. Feed her. Clothe her. Hold her. Just love her."

And with that, she walked into the house and came back out moments later with her bag, and without a word or a glance at me, she walked down the steps and headed to her car.

I should have called out.

Should have said something.

Like, what the fuck did she mean that the concept of love was foreign to me?

Chapter 9
Sutton

I felt like a coward as I fled from Irish's house.

But I couldn't help it.

After what he said that he didn't know how to do any of it, and with the things I gathered about his past, I was starting to see things clearly now.

And maybe, just maybe, he didn't realize how I felt about him.

And I knew that was true.

With each minute that passed.

So, I would need to tell him, at the same time I showed him.

With a plan in place, I crawled into my bed at the clubhouse and fell fast asleep.

The next couple of days passed by in a blur. I saw Irish when I could, and nine times out of ten, I was fast asleep on his couch when he walked in the door.

Sometimes, that was where I slept after he carried Maisie to her bed.

But not once did he carry me to his.

As that thought crept into my head, I began to wonder if I had made Irish out to be more than what he really was.

He didn't help me carry things.

He didn't let me sleep beside him.

He fucked me perfectly.

And he was there if I needed him

And he had killed two men for me.

But everything else?

He was nothing like Coal, and Pipe was to Adeline and Gabby.

And yes, I knew that they were their ol' ladies, but even before they made things official, they still treated them better than Irish did to me.

But my stupid heart didn't care about any of that.

I sighed as I ran my hand through the little girl's brown locks.

This right here was what every little girl dreamed of.

Having someone to be there for them.

To care for them.

To worry about any nightmares that may come for them in their sleep.

And to be there to chase them away.

I hadn't realized that Irish was home when I heard, "Is she sleeping?"

I smiled up at him and nodded.

He nodded, then moved to lift her, but I tagged his forearm and whispered, "Can we talk once you lay her down."

His eyes locked on mine; he took in a breath and nodded.

I waited on the couch for him to put Maisie in her bed.

When he came back, he toed off his boots and then sat down on the couch.

I waited for a beat, then I said, "Irish when I came to the clubhouse, I didn't know anyone. Or hardly anything. I lead with my heart. But when I became a club girl, I had no clue what was going to happen. I just knew I needed a safe space. To be allowed to learn who I am outside of that hell. And the club gave me that. You gave me that, Irish. So, I get it. Okay. I do. After the things I've seen with you and how you are, I get it. But I need to tell you, even though I've tried my best to show you. I'm in love with you. Totally in love with you."

He nodded.

He freaking nodded.

Umm. Okay.

What did that mean?

And then, he spoke, "You said that the concept of love was foreign to me, and you were right. I don't know how to love anyone. Never been loved, so how the fuck would I know?"

"But you have been, Irish. By your club brothers and by me. And soon by that little girl." I pleaded with him.

When he didn't reply, I said, "I want you, Irish. I want all of you. We connect. We understand each other. When you walk in a room, my breath hitches. I close my eyes at night, and it's you, I see. Do you know what I see when I look into your eyes? I see it all. I see everything. All my hopes. And all of my dreams. And I know you feel it, too. You have to."

I waited after pouring my heart out to him.

And I waited.

And I waited.

I was about to open my mouth to plead even more until he took the dagger he's always holding in his hand when it comes to me and plunged it into my heart, "I can't give you an answer, Sutton. I just can't."

How could he not see that my heart was in tatters at his feet?

I took in a breath and nodded.

Then I stood up because if I didn't get the fuck out of this house right now, I was going to scream.

And I would be damned if I woke Maisie up.

Then he called out, "Sutton?"

I took in a breath and looked at him, even when it hurt so fucking badly to do so.

"You'll still be there for Maisie. Right?"

I smiled weakly, "Yeah."

He whispered, "Thanks."

I nodded, trying to hide the hurt, but there was nothing I wouldn't do for that little girl, "Think nothing of it."

***

We were at the clubhouse a week later, and if it hadn't been a part of my contract for one more week, I wouldn't have shown up.

But I was there.

Present and unwilling, but I was there.

Maisie was at my side coloring a picture when Irish walked over.

Ever since I had told him how I felt, he had been distant.

If it didn't concern Maisie, we didn't talk.

He lifted his chin, "Have you got her?"

I lifted a brow, "Yeah, why?"

He didn't answer me.

No, all he did was nod and then head over to a certain table.

I felt my jaw drop.

Was he serious right now?

Surely, he wouldn't.... my heart dropped right out of my chest as I watched him offer her his hand, and then she licked her lips, placed her hand in his, and let him lead her into the clubhouse.

"Sutton?"

I tore my eyes from the now-empty doorway and looked down at the sweetest girl to ever grace this world, even though he had literally just torn my heart from my chest, I asked, "Yeah, Princess?"

"I gotta potty."

"Okay, sweet girl, let's go potty." She placed her hand in mine, and together, we headed into the clubhouse.

We returned to the courtyard and near the fire pit, all bundled back up underneath our blankets, when Asher took the chair to our right and asked, "Where's your man at?"

I shrugged, "I don't have a man."

Asher scoffed, "Yeah, fucking right. That boy made it clear you're his a few weeks ago when he laid Dawg out."

"Well, I told him how I felt about him. Laid my heart out, and he told me he couldn't say anything. That he just didn't know." I said through gritted teeth.

Seeing the arm that belonged to the man I wanted to call mine with every breath in my body curled around Cynammin's body, I wanted to scream.

But that would upset Maisie, and that was something I wouldn't allow to happen.

But something needed to change.

I just needed to get away for a little while. Figure out if I really wanted Irish in any way I could have him. And since I still had a week left on my contract, that would be up to Asher.

And with that thought firmly on my mind, I looked at Maisie, then I called out, "Asher?"

He looked at me and jerked his chin, "Right here, doll."

I looked into his gray eyes, "Do actions really speak louder than words?"

He took a deep pull from his cigar, "Yeah, they fuckin' do. Thought you knew that."

I shrugged, "I figured. I just wish my heart didn't feel as though someone took a pair of pruning shears to it. Ripped into it. And shredded it."

He growled, "Why?"

"Cause, Irish asked me if I had Maisie. And when I said that I did, like I always do, he went to her."

I didn't need to explain who the *her* was.

He knew.

Everyone knew.

"That fuckin' boy. He's going to fuck up and fuck up huge, and when he does, he's going to have nobody to blame but himself."

And when I saw how Pipe held onto Gabby and Coal held onto Adeline, I asked, "Think you can make some calls to another club for me? Not as a club girl. But just somewhere safe for me to gather my thoughts and get away from here?

Asher sighed, "Normally, I wouldn't do this kiddie shit. But he's made his own bed. It's time for him to lie in it."

I chuckled softly, "Kiddie shit?"

"Yeah, girl likes boy. Boy knows it. Boy thinks with his dick. Hurts the girl. Kiddie shit."

I chuckled softly again, fighting back the tears that wanted to streak down my cheeks.

I knew Asher saw it; he saw everything, and that was why he nodded and said, "I'll make some calls, darlin'."

"Thanks," I whispered, trying to hold back the tears that were threatening to fall.

Well, the first shoe dropped when he didn't say anything but what he did.

The second shoe dropped when he took that woman into the clubhouse.

And the third shoe... well... I was waiting for it.

Not with bated breath.

And I wouldn't know that the very next day it would happen.

***

I was at the stove making dinner at Irish's house.

Maisie was helping me pour the spices into the sauce.

And each time we did so, we made sounds to go with them.

I was laughing while she was giggling.

Neither one of us heard the front door open when she looked up at me and asked, "Sutton?"

I lifted a brow and looked at her, "Yeah, pretty girl?"

"Some kids get new parents when their old parents don't want them, don't they?"

I nodded, "Yeah, sometimes. Why do you ask?"

"Because since she didn't want me, and I know you want me, and I want you, think you can become my mommy?"

I didn't know what to say.

I'm honored.

I would love to.

I love you.

I was about to tell her that I didn't know because Irish had made it clear where I stood in his life... when he cleared his throat and said so nonchalantly, I was flabbergasted, "Sounds good to me. People co-parent all the time, right?"

How many more daggers could my heart take?

Then I ignored Irish, pain lacing my entire body, looked at Maisie, hid the hurt as best I could, and said, "I'd be honored to be your Mommy. Pretty girl."

She smiled wide, then flung herself in my arms. Oh, this sweet, sweet girl.

Oh, but the fuckery that was my life wasn't fucking over with... yet.

Chapter 10
Irish

I saw the hurt on Sutton's face when she tried to hide it, I truly did.

But I was still thinking about things.

Why did she want me?

That had been running through my head almost every single minute of every single day ever since she told me what she did.

But even though I couldn't figure out the situation between me and Sutton, I could do it for my daughter, and I would.

Even if I never claimed Sutton, she would always be Maisie's mother.

There was no one else on this earth that I had met in my thirty years of life who could do it better than she did.

We all gathered around the dining room table as I helped Sutton carry everything to the table.

I had just sat down when my phone rang.

I sighed, then pulled it out, and when I saw it was Cynnamin's name, I glared.

What the fuck was going on now.

I answered, "Cynnamin, what's going on?"

What I missed was that Sutton's body tensed.

Her teeth clenched.

And her hands fisted.

"I need your help. I'm close to doing it again. Can I come to you, Irish? Please?" If it weren't for the tears in her voice, I would have said no that she needed to confide in someone who was close to her.

I sighed, "Yeah, come on. Call me when you make it to the clubhouse. I'll meet you there." I said and then hung up the phone.

Sutton gasped, then her eyes narrowed, then she stood, stepped to Maisie's side, kissed her forehead, then she stepped to my side, opened her mouth, then closed it, and then she did something I never thought she would do.

She grabbed my plate that I had yet to touch, walked it over to the trash can, and dropped it in.

Then I sat there as I watched Sutton storm out of the house without a backward glance.

Then I looked at Maisie and asked, "Well, I guess she made her point, you want to share your food with me?"

She narrowed her eyes at me and tugged her plate closer to her chest.

Guess that answered that question.

Why? Why the fuck had I answered my damn phone?

Jesus Christ.

Why was I taking the woman that has been there for me for granted?

And as many times as I had asked myself that singular question.

I just keep fucking doing it.

Come the fuck on brain, make up your goddamned mind.

Either you fucking want Sutton, or you don't.

***

When my phone rang, I took the call, "Yeah?"

"I'm here," Cynammin said.

I nodded, then said, "Be there in fifteen."

Once I made it to the clubhouse, I headed to Sutton's room, hoping she wouldn't hold it against me right now, and thought about what I could say if she did.

Thankfully, or rather not, Sutton wasn't in there.

I sighed as I placed Maisie in Sutton's room, where she had things already there.

She snuggled into the blanket that Sutton used, sighed, and whispered, "I miss Mommy."

I knew she was talking about Sutton, and when I really thought about it, I realized that I did, too.

With Maisie tucked safely in Sutton's bed, I headed to my room and saw Cynnamin standing there with pale cheeks.

I sighed, unlocked my door, and held it open for her.

***

It was two hours later after I moved Maisie to my bedroom, I found myself on a stool at the bar. My brothers were drinking their drinks for their own reasons.

But I was drinking whiskey like it was water.

I couldn't keep hurting Sutton like I was.

She didn't fucking deserve it.

I thought as I took another shot.

And I didn't deserve her.

But fuck.

When the fuck would I ever find another woman like Sutton?

That would be never.

Because she was one of a kind.

Absolutely one of a fucking kind.

I closed my eyes, and then it hit me... her words... fucking everything. Seeing her in a wedding dress. My rings on her finger. Her name tangled with mine.

Why the fuck had I been pushing her away all these years?

Son of a bitch.

She was it for me.

The one.

My forever.

What I didn't know was that I should have stopped at the third drink... I hadn't.

And that was when my phone pinged with a text.

And when I got a look at the picture attached to the message. I. Saw. Fucking. Red.

But before I could fully process everything, I saw Maisie coming down the hall, at the same time, the front door opened, and there stood Sutton.

She looked at the bottle on the bar, then at the glasses, then looked at Maisie and sighed.

Sutton

I smiled at Maisie and said, "Come on, let's get you home."

"She's not going anywhere." I looked at Irish and watched as he narrowed his eyes.

I lifted a brow, "Why not?"

He sneered, what the fuck, "You're not taking my daughter anywhere."

"Your daughter?" I couldn't hide the hurt in my tone.

Slurring, he said, "Yeah. She's mine."

I glared, "You told me she was mine too."

He scoffed, "Didn't see you carrying her for nine months, Suuttttttonnnnn."

Maisie frowned and gripped my hand harder, "But daddy? You told me I could call Sutton mommy. So, I am hers."

He sneered, "Then she shouldn't have slept with Pagan and cheated on me."

I gasped, "What are you talking about?"

Cheated on him? Has he lost his ever-loving fucking mind?

If you look at it, he was the one cheating on me.

What a dickhead.

That was when he grabbed his phone, did something on it, and then showed me a picture of a woman with Pagan plowing into her.

What the fuck?

"I want you out of my life." Irish glared.

I lifted a brow and asked, "Were you drunk before or after you got that picture?"

"Nopppeeeee." He slurred.

And then it hit me: he was using this as an excuse to get rid of me. He knew how I felt about him.

But never mind that, he wasn't the man I thought he was. No, he was a coward.

Shaking my head, trying not to let the tears fall from my eyes, I dropped to my knees and pulled Maisie into my arms.

In her ear, I whispered, "I'm going to go away for a while, sweet girl. I don't want you to think that any of this is your fault. If you ever want to talk to me, all you have to do is ask Aunt Gabby or Aunt Adeline. Okay?"

She wiped the tears from her eyes, nodded, then wrapped her little arms around me and held me close, well as close as a five-year-old could manage.

Then I stood, wiping away my tears, and leveled my gaze at him, "You've gone too far this time, Irish. Too fucking far."

He sneered, "No, it's you who doesn't deserve me. I'm not the one whose damaged goods."

If they ever say their heart can't break anymore, well, then they haven't had their heart broken. Truly and utterly destroyed.

All around us, the men of Zagan MC started to growl; curses flew. Chairs were slammed back, and fists pounded on the bar and the tables.

With tears in my eyes, I asked, "Is that how you really feel? Why you won't make me yours."

He scoffed, "You were never meant to be mine. I wouldn't have someone like you raise my kid."

And with that said, he took another pull from his glass of whiskey.

I should have walked over to him and slapped him as hard as I could.

I should grab that glass and pour it over his head.

But I was done. I was so fucking done with this shit.

That was when I looked at Asher for the last time and asked, "Office?"

He nodded.

***

Once Asher gave me the details, I hugged him, thanked him, and took the ten grand he gave all the club girls once they finished their contract.

Then I walked out of his office, and with my chin held high, I went right to my bedroom and packed my things.

Thankfully, it hadn't taken me long.

The last thing I grabbed was Maisie's birthday present.

Then I walked out of my room with my things.

Then I looked at Rome and asked, "Where is Maisie?"

"In his room. That bitch is in Hallie's old room." He growled.

I nodded, then smiled at him.

But there was one thing I needed to say to Irish.

Stopping by the door, I turned then and said with a hollow tone, "That's funny. Didn't realize I have any tattoos."

And with that, I walked out of the main room, out the door, and to my car.

Blurred vision.

Tears coursing down my cheeks.

I made it to his house on autopilot.

Then I used my key, unlocked the door, headed to Maisie's room, and placed her birthday present on her bed.

Then I walked to the island, took the key off my key ring, and placed it on the island.

I didn't remember the drive to the Wrath MC Texas chapter's clubhouse.

Nor did I remember Cruz's face when he saw my red-rimmed eyes.

The last thing I remembered before my head hit the pillow in Cruz's room were the tears on Maisie's face.

Fuck. Him.

Chapter 11
Irish

Rolling over, I groaned.

Fuck I had too much whiskey last night.

Throwing my arms over my head to stretch, I felt a warm body next to mine.

Knowing that she was wet and ready for me, I rolled over and then froze.

That hair. That wasn't Sutton's.

Why was my daughter in bed with me and not at home with Sutton?

This was weird as fuck. Nothing had happened last night that I could remember.

Carefully getting out of bed, I walked to the en-suite bathroom.

Turning the water on hot, I stripped out of my clothes and climbed under the spray.

Just as I closed my eyes to let the water run down my body, I remembered everything that had happened yesterday.

And I fucking froze.

Then I unfroze, cut the water off, and hurried out of the shower, ignoring my body, leaving a trail of water from the bathroom to my nightstand, all the while also ignoring the nudity I was sporting, I tagged my phone.

Sutton's words to me last night had been, I *didn't realize I had any tattoos.*

The moment my eyes landed on the tribal sun tattoo on the back of the woman's shoulder, I all but sank to my knees.

Holy. Fucking. Shit.

Maisie lifted her head and blinked up at me, "Daddy, what's wrong?"

Grabbing a blanket, I covered my dick, ignoring my daughter, I called Sutton's phone.

It went straight to voicemail, and at the sound of her voice, I felt my heart fucking clench, "You've reached Sutton. Leave me a message."

As soon as it beeped, signaling to leave a message, I said, "Sutton. Baby. Please call me back. Fucking, please."

I ended the call and then looked at the photo again.

And that's when it hit me.

It definitely wasn't Sutton. How I had thought it was yesterday, I had no goddamn clue.

She had tattoos.

Her hair didn't have the same shine.

And that was when I read the message underneath the picture.

Pagan – *Fucking hell. Sorry man. Sent it to the wrong person. This bitch has been cheating on a friend of mine. He didn't believe me. So, I fucking showed him.*

Oh god.

I was this close to hitting my knees.

My eyes closed, remembering with vivid clarity the shit I had spewed at Sutton.

It was the tears in her eyes that I'll never forgive myself for.

It was the hurt look on her face that she didn't even try to hide.

I was a piece of shit.

Maisie wiped the sleep from her eyes when she asked, "Are you letting Mommy come back home?"

I nodded, "Yeah, cutie. As long as I can get her to accept my apology, I am. Then I'm making her my ol' lady and marrying her."

With the blanket around my bottom half, I checked to make sure she hadn't called back, then pressed a kiss on Maisie's forehead.

"Let daddy get dressed, then we will get you ready. Go potty right quick," I told her and then grabbed my clothes while she scrambled off the bed, ran around me, and pottied.

Fifteen minutes later, once we were both ready, I looked at the bedroom door. I've never dreaded walking out of my room and to the main part of the clubhouse ever in my life.

Not like I am this morning.

I remembered the looks my brothers gave me.

If I wasn't the man I am, it would have shriveled my balls.

But I wasn't a coward.

Far from it.

I kicked ass, and I took names.

And if I proved to Sutton that I was the right man for her, then by god, I would be the greatest man to ever walk the planet.

With Maisie's hand in mine, we walked down the hall, down the steps, and then we walked out of the clubhouse.

I felt the glares from my brothers, but I knew they wouldn't do or say anything with Maisie right there with me.

Once I got her safely ensconced in the truck I had bought a few weeks ago, we started looking for Sutton.

For hours and hours, we looked and nothing.

She wasn't at Coal and Adeline's place. She wasn't at Pipe and Gabby's place. Nor was she at Asher's.

But what freaked me out?

We went to the salon.

Sutton had canceled every appointment she'd made for at least six months.

I went to every single brother and asked if they knew where she was.

None of them would tell me.

Especially Asher.

I recalled her following him into his office, so I knew that he knew.

The fucker just wouldn't tell me.

After I dropped Maisie in my room at the clubhouse with what I now knew was the movie *Frozen*, I headed to the main room, got a cup of coffee, and waited.

***

My eyes kept watch on the clock.

I knew Gabby would know where Sutton was.

If Asher wouldn't tell me, then Gabby would.

The moment the door opened, and I saw Pipe with Gabby's hand in his, I stood up and then stormed over to where Gabby had just entered the clubhouse, "Gabby, where is she?"

She narrowed her eyes, then shrugged, "I can't tell you, Irish."

I growled, "Why the fuck not?"

Then she lifted her hand and counted down, "One, she asked me not to. Two, you're an asshole. Three, you don't deserve her. Four, she needs this time away from you. And five, you lost all respect in my eyes when you left Sutton to watch your daughter while you fucked that whore."

And with that, she let go of Pipe's hand and then shoulder-checked me and walked away.

I looked at Pipe, hope surely shone in my eyes, but he held his hand up, "I'm not going to risk pissing my woman off. I don't sleep unless she's next to me. Sorry, brother."

Just then, Asher came out of his office, leveled a glare on me, and snapped, "Church."

The moment the doors closed behind us in church, I slammed my hands on the table in church and growled, "You're my fucking brothers. Why the fuck are you taking her wishes over mine?"

Rome slammed his fist down and stood, pointed his finger at me, and said, "I'm tired of your shit, Irish. You've been told. You've been warned. Fucking hell, time and time a-fucking-gain that you were fucking up with that woman, but you didn't listen. You didn't give a flying fuck. I hope Sutton meets someone wherever she is that realizes that the moment, the very fucking moment he gets a look into the soft spot she has, that he knows he's just been given the world. And you had that. Just with a crook of your finger. You make me sick."

And with that, Rome stormed out of church. All without a backward glance.

As I took in the faces of my so-called brothers, I realized something.

They all felt the same fucking way.

Fuck.

Me.

Then the very last person I expected to say anything stood and then said, "You can go fuck yourself."

I watched as Coal stood and walked out as well.

And as he did so, everyone else stood too and walked out.

Asher sighed and then banged the gavel on the table.

"Irish, I warned you. Time and time again. What the fuck were you thinking?"

"I fucking wasn't, Pres. But goddamn."

A retort formed on the tip of my tongue along the lines of old habits that are hard to break, but I swallowed them down.

She didn't deserve that.

She didn't deserve to have a man who thought like that.

And when I found out she was gone, I had made a vow to be the man that deserved her.

And I would be that man. Come hell or high fucking water.

He sighed then, "Not sure I should tell you this, but if I was you, I'd want to know. Word got to me that a brother from another charter found out she was rid of you. He's making his claim on her. Soon."

"Then tell me, Asher. Tell me where she is so I can go get her and bring her home."

"You won't be able to bring that woman back here. Think about it, Irish. Think. She was raped by someone she should have been able to trust. And if that wasn't enough, the very first person she should have been able to count on, always, was the one who sat there and watched it all fucking happen."

I sat down in my chair then and dropped my head to my hands.

But Asher didn't let up, and if he had, I wouldn't have respected him as I should, "Then she gives her heart to you on a silver fucking platter, and you don't see it. Even though I know she's told you. She's told you so much that she loves you, it's a wonder those three words haven't lost all meaning for her. But then to watch her with Maisie and I know they haven't. She's shown you,

Irish, until she's been blue in the face. You want to know where she is, then fucking earn it."

I didn't know how. I would go about that.

What the fuck could I do to earn the information he held close to his chest.

Hell, the information that all my brothers held close to their chests, as well as their women.

I wouldn't know until almost two weeks later what I had to do.

And funnily enough, it had been the easiest thing I had ever done.

I was sitting beside Maisie, helping her color a picture of Minnie Mouse, her favorite, by the way, because she was Sutton's, too.

When the door to the clubhouse opened.

I lifted my head from the image and looked in that direction.

And when I saw it was the Soulless Outlaws, I dropped my head, knowing there was no danger, and kept coloring with my daughter.

It was only minutes later when I felt a hand trace the base of my neck, my entire frame tensed, and I pulled away, then jerked my head up to see who had dared to put their hands on me.

Because I knew it wasn't Sutton.

My body knew her touch, it fucking craved it.

And no one else would ever do.

Cynnamin stood there, smiling down at me, "It's been a long time, Irish. I need you. No one else has been able to satisfy me like you have."

I shook my head, "Can't. Go find someone else."

I looked back at the picture and started coloring again.

Cynammin sighed, "I see that you're busy, so I'll find you later."

When I felt her move, I said, "Don't bother. I'm spending the day with my daughter, then I'm going to bed," I bit back the words that I would be going to bed alone until I could get Sutton to forgive me.

Because Sutton didn't deserve to have me talking about her to this woman.

Not after the shit I had put her through.

Cynnamin frowned, "But any time I'm here, we always go to your bedroom. What's changed?"

I didn't know that we had the eyes and ears of everyone in the clubhouse not until after I said what I did and everything that unfolded after.

I looked down at Maisie and said, "Cover your ears, cutie."

I waited until she did just that.

Then I looked up at Cynnamin and said, "I know that. But shit has changed. I had the perfect woman in my life, and I was blind to it. Not anymore. She's the only woman for me. So again, like I said, you need someone to feed your habit, then go find someone else."

And that was all she would be getting from me about Sutton.

"Wait, is it the same woman who always looked sad anytime you headed off with me?" I didn't answer her.

She stood there.

Waiting.

But it was Maisie who I learned could still hear everything, and she proved that when she said, "My daddy already told you no. And he wants my mommy back. And I want her back, too. And he already knows that if he doesn't bring her back, I will never forgive him for it."

Jury came over then, the same fucker who I had knocked out for daring to ask Sutton if she wanted to head back to her room for some fun playtime, tagged Cynnamin's arm and pulled her away from the table.

I didn't watch where they went. My head just dropped to the picture I was coloring with Maisie.

Minutes later, her little arms wrapped around me as far as they could go, and she said, "I know you gotta work on getting Mommy back. You do that, and she still doesn't come home, I won't be mad at you. But if you ever go near that woman again, then I'll pull a Mommy and take your plate and throw it in the trash can."

I lifted my brow at her as she released her little arms and asked, "You will, will you?"

She nodded, "Yeah."

I smiled down at her and said, "You got a deal. Food is to be cherished; no way am I missing out on food."

She giggled, and then we finished the picture we were coloring.

It was after we had dinner, and she had taken her bath, that we settled in my room at the clubhouse when I asked, "What do you want to watch tonight?"

She smiled, "Frozen."

I nodded, then brought up the movie and pressed play.

My little girl was out in minutes.

And I was almost asleep moments later when there was a knock on my door.

My eyes moved to Maisie, and when I saw she was still sleeping, I got up carefully and walked to the door.

When I opened it a crack, it was to be met with Asher.

"Seen Cynnamin go off with two other men. See, you're settled for the night. See how you do while she's here." And with that cryptic as fuck statement, Asher walked away.

I sighed, then shook my head and headed back to bed.

Within minutes, I was out, but not before I whispered, "I'm going to find you, baby. And if you don't want to come back, then me and Maisie will be following you. Anywhere you wish to go, we will be right there with you."

The next day, after I got Maisie ready and dropped her off at Adeline and Coal's house, I had just planned the route for the next gun shipment we were dropping off when I walked into the garage and got started on a few of the repairs that had come in overnight.

It was two hours later when the air in the garage shifted.

I frowned, lifted my head out from under the hood I was working, and looked out of the open bay.

Cynnamin was standing there, her hands on her hips, and when she saw me, she dropped her hands and then walked over to where I was.

The moment she reached me, she said, "Those two guys last night wouldn't help me. I need you, Irish. Surely, these cars can wait. I can't."

"You are not her. I won't say it again, Cynnamin. No other woman is getting any part of me but her. She has all of me. So do me a favor and get the fuck away from me. And stay the fuck away from me, or else you'll be banned from all Zagan MC properties."

Nuke spoke then, "You want me to go further, your ass will be kicked out of Soulless Outlaw's MC properties as well. And since we got allies, you won't find any refuge with Wrath MC, Immoral Saints, or Pagan's Soldier's MC. And seeing as we dominate the south, you'll need to move up north. He's told you he's claimed. You don't step on that. Ever. Don't test me."

It was half an hour later or so when Asher walked into the garage, came straight to me, and dropped a piece of paper on my toolbox.

"Don't fuck this up." And with that, he turned on his boot and walked away.

My fingers trembled as I tagged the slip of paper, knowing what was on it by his words last night and just now.

When I saw the address, I automatically calculated how far away she was.

An hour later, after I was packed, I first texted Asher.

I needed an emergency club meeting, and if it took divulging a secret for a secret, then I would do it for my woman. I would break anything for that woman, including my word.

But I would never break it... for her.

Once everyone was in church and Asher banged the gavel, he said, "Irish has called an emergency meeting. Let's hear him out."

I nodded at him, then took in a breath... "Six years ago, Cynnamin was violently attacked almost as bad as Shiloh was. You all know that story. And ever since then, she has had a kink of sorts. She hates it, but with help, she's learned to deal with it."

I took in a breath, "Cynnamin enjoys telling someone what to do while they say no. She called me one night, crying because she had a man in her bed, and he told her no, and she didn't listen. So, I offered to be that person for her. We don't touch ever. She just tells me what to do with my body while I say no. I feel like I owe her. You all know I bounced around from foster home to foster home."

They nodded in unison.

"What I didn't tell you was that I hate, and I mean I hate, fucking sweet peas. They look like puke when they are overcooked. And one night, in one of the foster homes, I refused to eat them. The man didn't like that. Cynnamin covered my body when the man started to beat me. She took the beating that was meant for me. Had she not done that, I would have been seriously injured, I was seven at the time and she was thirteen."

None of them reacted, even though looks of shock marveled all their faces.

"Not once have I ever touched Cynnamin like that. And she has never touched me like that. I swear that on my kutte, my club, my life, that of my daughter's, and on Sutton's."

It was Stoney who exploded, "You let us give you so much shit, boy. What the fuck for?"

I simply said, "I promised her. I gave her my word."

"Fuck. I gave you so much shit," Pipe said.

I lifted my chin, "Don't mention it. Had I really been doing what you all thought I had been doing, I would have expected nothing less."

Rome held up his thumb and middle finger, "I was this close to putting a bullet in you."

"If I had done that, I would have deserved it. She's the last one I ever want to hurt."

"We got your back. Whatever you need." Asher said.

I nodded.

Once I shared everything, I went to Adeline and Coal's house, and when Maisie came skipping out, I dropped to my haunches and said, "I'm going to go talk to Mommy. I'll be gone a few days, a week at most. You'll be okay with Adeline and Uncle Coal?"

My little girl put her hands on her hips and said, "You'll be gone however long it takes to bring Mommy home."

I smiled at my girl, "I'll do my best, but I gotta grovel to your Mommy. Okay?"

She sighed then, "I want to ask, but I'll wait to find out what grovel means."

Adeline laughed, then offered Maisie her hand, "I'll tell you what it means, okay?"

Maisie nodded, then pressed a kiss on my cheek and walked with Adeline into their house.

Coal spoke then, "You need me to go with you?"

I shook my head, "You're guarding the other half of my heart. So, I know she's safe. I gotta fight for the other part of my heart. Rather not have y'all see me get my ass kicked and ride with me with my tail tucked between my legs."

"It'll be hard," he said, then looked in the direction of the house where his own world had just walked into, then looked back at me, "but so fucking worth it."

I nodded, knowing he was right.

Then, I climbed on my bike and headed to Texas. Bradford Valley, to be exact.

Where one of the charters of Wrath MC was located.

I was grateful, honestly, that she had gone there.

Yes, every club of Wrath MC was safe, as were all our allied clubs... but for a group of active Special

Forces, there was only one safer place for her to be, other than my arms.

This was going to be a long ride, almost eleven hours, but if I needed to drive to Alaska to grovel, then I would.

If I needed to travel through the Bermuda Triangle to get to her, then I would do that, too.

***

I made the drive to Austin, Texas, in eleven hours.

I was beat.

But nothing compared to the way my heart felt when I remembered in vivid detail the pain on my woman's face.

And she was that.

My woman.

As I pulled into the compound, I stopped at the gate.

And before I could say a word, the six men filed out of a building that was hidden to the outside.

Cruz, Teague, Waylon, Miller, Trajen, and Raj.

Cruz crossed his arms over his chest and glared, "She needs time. Leave."

I shook my head. "No. You don't know her like I do. What she needs is for me to tell her how I really feel. How I was too fucking stupid to realize what I had in front of me."

"And it's my understanding that everyone tried to tell you about that, but you wouldn't fucking listen. Now, you lost her. Sucks to be you." Teague rumbled out.

Then, at the same time, Raj pulled a knife from the back of his jeans and started spinning it, blade first, in his hands.

"I'm not leaving until I talk to her. To see her." I told them, enforcing my determination in my tone.

Cruz smirked, "And that's why you won't see her."

I narrowed my eyes, "Come again?"

"You were told she needs time. But once again, you don't give a damn about her, you only care about yourself. Now get." Cruz growled.

"I'm not leaving until I have eyes on her. You wanna keep me from her, you go ahead, but I promise you, I'll take two of you with me as I go." I told them.

Not caring that I just threatened them. Not in the fucking slightest.

Then, I caught sight of the most beautiful woman I'd ever seen in my life.

She was pissed.

Oh yeah.

She was livid.

And with every step, as she grew closer to me, she stomped.

"How dare you show up here after the shit you pulled and said. Get the fuck out of here." She screamed.

"Sutton, baby, we need..." I stopped talking.

Because she hissed, "Don't you dare tell me what we need, you motherfucking asshole. Those men were horrible to me. But no one has ever had the power to break me. You want a medal for doing it? I'll have one made and sent to you. You can show your new woman that you're a real fucking winner. You're a real motherfucking prize." And with that, she turned on her foot and walked back into a building.

I growled, clenched my fists, and deep breathed.

"Damn. I'd hate to feel what you're feeling. Good thing I'd never treat a woman like Sutton the way you did." Waylon said.

Then, all at once, they left.

I had half a mind to ram the gate.

But I would fuck up my bike.

But did it really matter?

My bike or her...

No... there was no comparison.

I thought about doing it, even backed and revved my engine to do it, until I saw something and then looked down at my chest.

A red dot was hovering center fucking mast.

I dropped my head, then sighed, then whispered, "I'll be back. I'm going to win you back, baby."

I found a hotel and got a room, and then I crashed.

Unfortunately, I was only able to get about four hours of sleep because I woke up while remembering the look on Sutton's face as I hurled that shit at her.

After I showered and got dressed, I packed up the room, checked out, and headed back.

I sat on my bike in the blistering sun for six hours.

I felt eyes on me, but I didn't move.

Sutton knew a lot about me.

But she didn't know how stubborn I could be when I really wanted something.

I had just taken a sip of water when I saw movement.

Sutton.

My world.

My heart.

She reached the gate, put her hands on her hips, and asked, "If I hear you out, will you leave?"

I nodded, "Yeah. Please, baby."

She sighed and then waved her hand.

The gate started to move then, and as I walked my bike in, she said, "Follow me."

I did.

When we stopped at a brick building, I dismounted and then followed her in.

All six men were sitting there, their weapons on the tables, just waiting.

I warned them, "I won't stand still for y'all to shoot me. But I will for Sutton."

Sutton scoffed, then rolled her eyes, mumbling, "Yeah, fucking right."

Fuck. But I had broken her. She never would have reacted to me like that.

"Where's Maisie?" she asked.

And that.

That right there was why I had been one dumb fucking son of a bitch.

She didn't ask about anyone else.

She didn't check in on Gabby, Adeline, Stella, or Chloe.

No, she only wanted to know about Maisie.

"She's okay. She's with Adeline."

She nodded, then crossed her arms over her chest and sighed, "Why are you back here, Irish?"

"Because you're here. And Maisie told me that if I didn't bring you back to her, she would hate me forever."

She snickered, "That's my girl."

"Yeah. She is from the roots of her hair to the tips of her toes. She's all yours, baby. And so am I."

When she didn't respond to that, I asked, "You won't come back? Not even for Maisie?"

She sighed, "I love her. I do. But I think she's gathered that if her father wasn't a blind asshole, then I wouldn't have ever left."

"And you're right. One hundred percent right. I was a blind asshole. But baby, my eyes are wide fucking open now. And if you'll give me another chance, I promise you, I won't let you down. You can count on me. Give me your worries, your fears, your hopes, your dreams, and I'll carry it all for you. I'll shelter you from any storm."

She didn't respond.

No, what she did was rip me to shreds when she asked, "How many women have you been with?"

I winced, "Sutton, please, don't do this."

"Answer me." She snapped.

I ran my hand through my hair, locked eyes with her, and said, "Too many to count."

And I've never felt lower than shit as I did right then.

Standing there in the main room of some building in the Bradford Valley clubhouse, watching as the woman who was the light of my life, tears streaming down her pale cheeks.

"Exactly. It wasn't me who didn't deserve you. It was you who didn't deserve me." And with those final words I had thrown in her face, she placed her hands on my chest and shoved me out the door. And I went willingly because there was no way I would ever do bodily harm to her.

And with that, she closed the door in my face.

And I stood there; my heart felt as though it were breaking into a million pieces.

My knees went weak, but I gritted my teeth.

I would be damned if anyone saw me hit my knees other than Sutton.

It was time for round two.

I was going to be known as the man who never stopped fighting for what he wanted and what he needed.

Challenge accepted, baby.

I drove back home and then spent a week getting everything ready.

I replaced her wardrobe in my closet.

Had her a set of keys made.

Had adoption papers made.

Rings made.

The form for a marriage license.

And I had her property kutte made.

When Maisie saw all of this, she clapped.

I was hoping this would work because if it didn't... I didn't know what I would do.

I also went to Hugo, a badass tattoo artist at Badd Motha Ink, and had him create a design that takes up the entirety of my left chest.

All with Sutton's name right in the middle, visible for the world to see.

A week later, I made the drive again.

And I sat out on my bike for two hours this time when the gate moved, and Sutton came out, threw her hands in the air, and growled, "What fucking now?"

I grinned and then walked my bike in again.

Once I dismounted, I grabbed one of the black saddlebags.

Then I followed her inside.

Walking to a table, I began pulling stuff out of the black saddle bag.

First came out her property kutte.

Followed by the box that held her ring.

Next, the marriage license form.

Followed by the adoption papers.

Then I pulled out her set of keys. One to my house, one to my truck, one to the garage, and one to my room at the clubhouse.

Then I gestured, "Everything on the table is yours. I am yours. Maisie is yours. Forever."

Then she crossed her arms over her waist and whispered, "Nothing's changed, Irish. Nothing."

I nodded, "Everything has changed. My eyes are wide fucking open, baby. Fucking wide."

"And that woman?" she asked. Hatred in every word.

Then I repeated the same words to Sutton that I had told my brothers because I knew them by fucking heart.

"Six years ago, Cynnamin was violently attacked. And ever since then, she has had a kink of sorts. She hates it, but with help, she's learned to deal with it."

I took in a breath, "Cynnamin enjoys telling someone what to do while they say no. She called me one night, crying because she had a man in her bed, and he told her no, and she didn't listen. So, I offered to be that person for her. We don't touch ever. She just tells me what to do with my body while I say no. I feel like I owe her. You all know I bounced around from foster home to foster home."

She didn't react.

"What I didn't tell you was that I hate, and I mean I hate, fucking sweet peas. They look like puke when they are overcooked. And one night, in one of the foster homes, I refused to eat them. The man didn't like that. Cynnamin covered my body when the man started to beat me. She took the beating that was meant for me.

Had she not done that, I would have been seriously injured, I was seven at the time and she was thirteen."

Tears welled in her eyes, at what I said. But she didn't open her mouth, nor did she make a move to pull me into her arms as she had done so many times before.

And why wouldn't she?

Because every time she did that, I was the dumb fuck that pushed her away.

"That's the god's honest truth, Sutton. Not once has she ever touched my body like that. And not once have I ever touched her body. I swear to you. Just the thought of touching her makes my balls shrivel up. She does nothing for me in that way. Only you do."

And when she didn't react to that statement, I gathered every bit of pride I held onto and made sure Sutton was my only focus as I dropped to my knees right in front of her.

With my eyes looking up into her eyes that hold all my dreams, I said, "This should tell you things about me. This should show you."

She lifted a brow, "Show me what?"

"I don't go down on other women. Only you." I told her, pouring every ounce of honesty into my words that I could.

She scoffed, "And that's supposed to make me feel better?"

Seeing that what I was doing wasn't working, I stood up and then crowded into her space, ignoring the growls from Cruz, Waylon, Teague, Miller, Trajen, and Raj.

I brought my hand up and cupped the side of her neck, "Baby, a man will only drop to his knees for the woman who holds his heart in the palm of her hand."

She rolled her eyes, then stepped out of reach and asked, "Are you finished? Get everything out you wanted to say?"

I swallowed, then nodded, "Yeah, but two things."

She sighed, "And those are?"

"I'm sorry for every single time I hurt you. And I love you. I love you so fucking much, Sutton. It's a wonder I can feel my heart beating."

And with that, she nodded, "I appreciate you apologizing, but that's not enough. I don't think anything ever will be."

And with that, she walked out of the building.

The six men stood then, and Cruz said, "Time for you to go."

I was stubborn, but my woman seemed to be even more stubborn.

But the ball was in her court, and I would be here for her, no matter fucking what.

Chapter 12
Sutton

I had just washed the last breakfast dish after the men told me I didn't have to cook or clean.

And then they all yelled at me that since I cooked, I shouldn't have to clean.

Why couldn't I have met one of them before I met Irish?

Damn.

But then a thought crept into my head.

He killed men for me.

Two.

Wasn't that worth something?

I shook my head, and then, as I dried my hands, my phone on the counter rang.

When I saw it was Asher, I smiled, then answered, "Hey."

His smokey voice came over the line, and I knew he had a cigar in his hand, "Hey, sweetheart. How's things?"

I shrugged, even though he couldn't see me, "Things are okay. I'm still trying to get my bearings."

"Yeah, I get that." He was silent.

And so was I.

Then I heard him sigh, "I'm going to tell you something. I need you to give me some respect and listen. Alright?"

It was my turn to sigh, but I did respect Asher. A hell of a lot. So, I said, "Okay."

"He's hurting, Sutton. I know he hurt you. I do. But he's a good man once he pulls the 'whatthefuckamIdoing' stick out of his ass. He wouldn't be my brother if he wasn't a good man. Give him another chance, Sutton. If he breaks your heart or lets you down one more time, I'll put a bullet in him myself."

I grinned at the thought, but... "But you've watched him, Asher. You've watched everything. You're the first person to tell anyone who will listen that if you give someone a chance and they blow it, then they're not worth your time."

I heard him sigh then, "Yeah, I know. But I know Irish, Sutton."

And with that, he disconnected.

And over the next week, I did nothing but think.

But in those three weeks.

Packages showed up at the clubhouse.

Jewelry.

Chocolates.

Thick, warm socks.

Spa kits.

You name it, it arrived.

Even the men thought it was funny at first until they had to haul everything to the room I was staying in.

And then a package came.

It was a letter from Maisie.

'Mommy, I miss you. I know Daddy messed up. I don't understand all that happened, but at night, when Daddy thinks I've gone to bed, I heard him crying. And one time, I saw him holding a picture of you. The same picture he put on my bedside table. Daddy also had the house redecorated, and he bought you new stuff. It's all in the house. But if you don't come home, then I'm talking Daddy into bringing me next time when he comes to see you. I love you, Mommy. And I miss you."

And at the bottom of the letter, read.

'We miss you too, Sutton. So much. We want you to come home. Forgive him. Please. And I wrote the letter. Irish has no clue about it. – Adeline.

After I read the letter, I folded it up and put it in my memory box.

Then I closed the lid and sat down on my bed.

And then, I didn't even try to stop the tears that trailed down my cheeks or the broken sob.

I didn't even hear a knock on the door.

Nor did I see Raj poke his head in.

But I found myself in his arms as I cried big freaking tears.

His only words to me were, "You got your miracle. He manned up. Give him a chance. Alright?"

It was the very next day when I came in from riding four-wheelers when I pulled out my phone and saw that I had a voicemail.

After I hit the button and brought the phone to my ear, my breath hitched at his ragged tone.

'I love you, Sutton. Fuck. But I love you. Me and Maisie are here waiting for you. And if you never want to come here, then me and Maisie will come to you. I'll work as a janitor, as a fry cook, I don't give a fuck. Not as long as I have you. And you have me. I want my family. Me, you, and Maisie, so take your time, alright. We aren't going anywhere.'

Irish

Seeing the sadness on my baby girl's face all but did me in. Today was her birthday. And she had let me know right quick that she wasn't having a party if Sutton couldn't be here.

So, I didn't order the cake.

I didn't hang the decorations in the house that Sutton had bought.

I curled up with my daughter; her soft snores were hilarious, but I just couldn't smile.

I haven't smiled since I smiled at Sutton when I tried to get her to forgive me.

Maisie had just snored again when there was a timid knock at my door.

Sutton

I stood there, waiting, and when the door opened, I stared up at him.

Has he been eating?

My word.

Even his eyes looked sunken in.

He had dark circles around his eyes, too.

And the usual vibrant gray eyes were dull. Oh. No.

But then I saw a small spark in them when his eyes looked me up and down, and he whispered, one broken word, "Baby?"

At his tone, I simply asked, "Did you mean it?"

"Meant every fucking word." He growled at me.

Just then, I heard, "Mommy?"

Stepping around him, I stepped into the house, and then the moment Maisie saw me, I watched as excitement rippled across her face before she jumped off the couch, bringing my heart in my throat and then running full tilt towards me.

I dropped to my knees, and the moment she made it to me, I wrapped my arms around her and pulled her in as close as I could.

Her face went into my neck while I inhaled her scent. It was all Maisie.

I stood up with her as she wrapped her legs around my waist, clinging to me like a freaking spider monkey.

Then I looked at Irish. "You're done with her. Right?"

He nodded. "Totally done with her. Never again, baby. You're it for me."

I looked into his eyes, looked deep, and saw it there.

Truth. Honesty. And the newest emotion... love.

I smiled.

"Think you could kiss..." I got nothing else out.

Because his arms wrapped around the two of us, pulling us into his chest, and then his lips came down on mine.

His touch was like a feather, light at first, but then when his tongue delved into my mouth, I tried my hardest to bite back the moan, but I hadn't accomplished it.

When we pulled away, he was breathing heavily, and so was I.

His forehead rested on mine, and then he whispered, "Is my woman home?"

I smiled and then nodded, "But... you hurt me one more time, Irish, whatever the rest of your name is, and I won't allow Asher to kill you. I'll do it myself."

He winked, "Deal. And it's Michael Elias White"

I grinned.

Then I walked further into the house and frowned, "Where's the cake and the decorations?"

Irish wrapped his arms around us again and said, "She didn't want to have a party without you here."

I nodded, then looked at Maisie, "You still want that party?"

She bit her lip and nodded.

I grinned, "Okay, pretty girl."

I sat her down on her feet and said, "You open the gift I left on your bed?"

She grinned, then nodded.

I nodded back, "Go put it on for me, okay?"

"Okay, Mommy." And just like that, she took off like a shot.

I smiled. Damn, but I had missed hearing that.

Then I called the girls.

Ten minutes of us talking and them saying they were so happy I was home, and then they said they would be right over, and they would put the word out about Maisie's party.

Once I hung up the phone, I was back in Irish's arms.

His lips were on mine, "Tonight, I'll show you how happy I am that you're home."

I smiled, "Good. I look forward to it."

He grinned, then he sobered, his eyes staring intently into mine, and then he asked, "Will you give me an answer, Sutton?"

I tilted my head to the side, "An answer? To what?"

"Everything I left with you," he said.

I shook my head, "I need time, Irish. I have to be able to trust you again. Is that okay?"

He nodded, "Yeah, baby. It's more than okay. Long as I have you, I don't give a fuck."

And yes, Maisie's party went off without a hitch.

The men of Zagan MC all gave me hugs, but Creature didn't. And that was okay. I still didn't know much about him, other than some shit went down, and he had to leave. He went nomad.

But what had me laughing my ass off was the fact that with every single one of those hugs, Irish growled and cursed.

But he cursed low so Maisie couldn't hear it.

And the men and women of Zagan MC had given her every present known to man that would make any little girl deliriously happy.

Even though she remained glued to my side, and later that night, Irish didn't get to show me how happy he was that I was home.

And that was due to the little girl who was now six years old and didn't want to be separated from me for even a nanosecond.

And yes, true to everything, Irish had bought me a new wardrobe, and I was wearing a T-shirt that had his last name on the back of it.

But... he did show me how happy he was that I was home the very next day after Adeline and Coal picked her up to go spend some of her birthday money.

Chapter 13
Irish

After I showed Sutton how happy I truly was that she was home, I carried my woman's things into the house. I smiled then. The first genuine smile to hit my face in weeks.

And for the rest of the week, Maisie wound up in our bed at night.

Sutton didn't mind.

And I sure as hell didn't mind.

Especially not when Sutton rolled into my side, cuddled close, and then let out one of her little sighs, I couldn't help the smile that split my face in two.

Finally.

Fucking finally.

With my little girl cuddled to my side and my woman at my other side, I finally felt whole.

And I hadn't felt that since I was four years old and watched my parents pull away from where I stood at the Fire Department.

***

We were at the clubhouse planning out the Christmas festivities when all of a sudden, Charlie ran into the main room with his tablet in his hand and made a beeline straight for me, "I found him, I fucking finally found him. That limp dick motherfucker."

It took me a moment to figure out who he was talking about, and then it hit me.

Fucking finally.

I already took care of that motherfucker, Gerard, he pissed himself. Thankfully, none of it had gotten on my person.

We've been searching for that slimy bastard for well over a year now, and somehow, he's always been one step ahead of us.

Well, not anymore motherfucker.

Two hours later, I, along with Asher, Coal, Pipe, Priest, Stoney, Whit, Charlie, Rome, Creature, Pagan, and Trigger, rode out.

He was one dumb motherfucker for returning to his home, but I was glad for it.

We didn't slow until we pulled in front of his house.

Asher locked eyes with everyone, and since we had all done this dance more times than either of us could count, it was child's play.

But before we moved in, every single one of us pulled on a pair of black leather gloves that would be burned.

We were like wraiths there to claim souls and gift them to the Reaper as we moved through the house on silent feet.

The moment we reached his study, I opened the door and smiled at him from where he sat behind a desk.

Sweat was visibly beading on his forehead.

"The authorities have been called. I don't know who you all are, but you've come to the wrong house." He said.

"Oh yeah?" I asked with a grin.

"Yes, whatever you came to do, I can assure you, you won't get away with it." He said, his hand clenched into a fist atop his desk.

I tilted my head to the side, "What would they think about you ordering your very own stepdaughter to be raped and then sat there and watched it happen?" I asked.

The fucker had the audacity to snap and say, "I don't know what you're talking about, the little bitch obviously lied."

The sound of a hammer clicking before a spot of crimson could be seen on the man's white dress shirt, Rome said, "No one calls that woman a bitch.

"I'm only going to share two things with you about her. One, she stopped having nightmares a week after she came to the clubhouse because she realized that Gerard was nothing but a pussy, and I would be damned to allow him to breathe for a minute longer."

Raymond Frederick Stanton, the fucking IV, gasped and paled, "That was you?"

I grinned, "I may not be the enforcer or the Icer for my club, but nobody hurts a woman like that and lives to talk about it."

The man didn't respond. Good.

Because I had one more thing to say before I killed him.

I moved forward, and as I did, more guns were produced and aimed at the bastard.

With my arm, I swept everything that was on his desk onto the floor.

And then I shared, "She's good. She's smiling. She's happy. She's my ol' lady and soon to be my wife. And she's a mother. A damn good mother. Just like her mother was."

And with that, I said, "You're the last person alive who's seen my woman's wonderful body. And you're about to be taking your final breaths."

That was when the bastard started to grasp for straws.

We wouldn't be having that.

"I'll give you anything you want. Name your price," he pleaded.

I smiled, "Your price is death."

Then I stepped around him and hauled his body atop the desk.

Then I looked at Rome and Coal, "Hold him down for me?"

They moved in, Rome took his arms, and Coal took his legs.

Then I looked at Creature, "You got it?"

He nodded, then pulled something from his back pocket while I ripped the piece of shit's shirt open.

Creature moved to the fireplace that was already lit and ready to be used, good man.

Once Creature had the item good and hot, he handed it to me.

I grinned, then took the branding iron and smiled down at the piece of shit.

Then, I didn't hesitate to press it into the man's bare chest.

His cries of pain were like the sweetest notes I'd ever heard, but nothing compared to the sounds of my woman and my little girl.

Once the scent of burning flesh filled the room, I removed the branding iron.

And there, on his chest, read two words, "Cunt Waffle."

I handed the branding iron back to Creature, and then I pulled my knife from the waistband of my jeans, and then I moved.

With the knife, I carved his eyes from their sockets and then tossed them to the ground, and for good measure, while he was screaming and writhing in pain, I stomped on them.

With that done, I sneered at the bastard, "You know, I think you're a pussy. Because I watched a man lose his hand, and not once did he utter a sound but did grit his teeth. Now that I think about it, I want to find out."

Then I used that same knife and cut at the material he was wearing until I revealed his boxers.

Then I cut that material away until his small pencil dick could be seen.

I laughed at the sight of it, as did my brothers.

And then, once I sobered up, I said, "I wish Sutton's mother never would have met you. One, she wouldn't be left unsatisfied after you put that small fucking eraser in her. But then again... I may never have met Sutton. That would have been a travesty because she's the air I need to breathe."

Then I smiled, and with my gloved hand, I moved his eraser... umm, his dick out of the way, and then I cut his balls from his body.

Then I looked at Creature, "Think you can go find me a towel?"

He nodded, then left the room and returned moments later with a white one. Fucking funny.

"Umm, Irish, what the fuck are you doing?" Pipe asked.

I looked at him, then looked at the rest of my brothers who had come with me, and said, "It's my birthday present to Sutton."

Then, I grabbed a white towel, dropped the fucker's balls in it, and wrapped it up.

Then and only then, through the man's bellowed rages of pain, I wiped my knife off, then pulled my gun out and said, "This was all for Sutton. There's no limit to the depths of depravity I won't go to for her."

Then I fired my gun, as did the rest of my brothers.

In a split second later, the man stopped breathing.

Then I ransacked through his office and fired at the safe.

Once I got it open, I looked through it.

And when my eyes landed on the ruby-red tennis bracelet. I grinned.

With the package for Sutton in my hand, I walked into the clubhouse, scanned the room for my gorgeous woman, and made a beeline for her.

Thankfully, Maisie wasn't in there.

"Happy early birthday, Sutton," and with that, I laid the towel-wrapped gift in front of her.

She scrunched her nose, "What is it?"

"Hang on, I'm not done," I told her as I pulled the bracelet that was her mother's out of my pocket.

I tagged her wrist and then slid it on.

She had tears running down her cheeks, but I grinned, and then I tilted my head to the towel.

"Now. Open it and find out," I told her.

Whit walked over and said, "If you've just eaten anything, I wouldn't do it."

She gagged, "Oh, Jesus. Irish, what is it?"

I smirked, "Finally found the fucker. Your stepfather." Then I tilted my head to the towel-wrapped gift, "I brought you his balls."

She sat there. Stunned.

Then she threw her head back and roared with laughter.

I just stood there and watched.

I knew I would get her back.

There was no other outcome I would ever accept.

But then she sobered, looked up at me, and whispered, "Yes."

It took my brain a minute.

But then... I hollered, "Maisie!"

She came running and gasped, "Daddy?"

"Let's go get married," I said, then I bent and wrapped an arm around Sutton, tossed her over my shoulder, and strode for the door.

All the while, Maisie clapped and giggled and walked to my side.

My woman was laughing her ass off.

Three hours later, I kissed my wife for the first time.

And fifteen minutes later, in a courthouse bathroom, I made love to my wife for the first time.

It was one week before Christmas when there was a knock on the door.

"I'll get it," I called out to my girls as I made my way to the front door.

When I opened it, I stared at some woman standing there.

Jeans, a white sweater, and dark brown hair.

I lifted my brow, "Can I help you?"

"I'm ready for us to be a family. I want my kid back, and I want you." She stated.

Sutton heard what the woman said. I knew that, because in the next instant, she was around my body.

Her arm pulled back, and she slammed it into Kendra's nose.

Blood splattered everywhere.

She snapped, "That was for sleeping with Irish."

And then she backhanded Kendra so hard that I was glad as fuck I never pissed her off. Because I winced.

"That was for abandoning that little girl outside of the gates where she was unprotected, you fucking bitch."

Thankfully, my brothers pulled up at just the right time.

Kendra screeched again, "She's my daughter."

But it was Creature who said, "No. She's Sutton's."

Just then, the brothers grabbed her by the arms and hauled her off our front porch.

Gabby and Adeline came in then and smiled, Adeline nodded, "We got her, we're going to make cookies. Go do your thing and slap that woman for me?" she asked as she looked at Sutton.

Sutton winked, then headed out to my bike, determination in every step, but my eyes were glued to her ass.

Fuck, I was one lucky son of a bitch.

Needless to say, I had to fuck my woman in the kitchen in the clubhouse, I couldn't wait to get her up to our room.

Not after my woman beat the holy hell out of the woman before every brother in the MC put bullets in her body.

Things were great, so great, I was still kicking my ass for never really seeing what I had.

But I would never be that fool again.

Sadly, the day before Christmas Eve, Sutton's phone rang.

Chapter 14
Sutton

With my hand in Irish's and my other hand held by Maisie, he led us to my SUV.

Once Maisie was all buckled in, he opened my door.

Once I was settled, he leaned in, swept his thumb over my cheek, and said, "You need me, you flash your lights, alright?"

I smiled weakly, then nodded.

Then, after Irish closed my door, I heard, "Mommy, I'm right here if you need me. Okay?"

I turned around in my seat and smiled at my girl, "Thank you, baby."

I took in a deep breath, and then I turned my SUV on, my Christmas present from Irish.

When we pulled up outside of the cemetery, I wanted to laugh at all the shocked stares the men of Zagan MC received. But also that of Soulless Outlaws, Pagan's

Soldiers, Immoral Saints, Wrath MC, the Alabama chapter, and the Texas chapter.

But I didn't.

Instead, I cut my SUV off, unbuckled, climbed out, and got Maisie out.

Just as I was shutting her door, a steely arm wrapped around my waist and pulled me to his front.

His face lowered, pressing itself into the side of my neck, his lips brushing the skin there as he asked, "You okay, baby?"

I nodded, then wrapped my free hand around his that was resting against my stomach, "Yeah, I won't be later. But right now, I am."

***

We all stood there as the little girl's casket was lowered into the ground.

The headstone read *Paisley Marie Combs. Beloved Daughter. Friend. Gone too early, but never forgotten.*

As soon as everyone left, we surrounded Holly.

The girls and I wrapped her in hugs, Adeline looked at her, "Whenever you need girl time, we are always here for you."

***

We had invited Holly to spend the holidays with us because she didn't need to be alone.

Paisley was all she had left in the whole world.

Thankfully, she had decided to celebrate the holidays with us.

But I had a bad feeling about it.

We were going to have to keep a close watch on her.

And sadly, I had been right.

Holly hadn't been able to cope with the death of Paisley, and I doubted that if I were to lose Irish and Maisie, I would have done the same thing she did.

She slipped away peacefully the very night after Christmas.

It was a month later, as I walked out of the salon, when I saw something sitting on the hood of my car.

Four white doves.

Mom Dad, Holly, and Paisley.

I didn't have to second guess that or question it, I just knew.

I lifted my head to the sky, and I smiled. "Thanks, Mom."

But that wasn't the only thing that rocked our world, or rather mine.

No, after Irish had disposed of my stepfather, and the MC had killed the men, a certain someone showed up at the clubhouse.

And if I hadn't been watching it with my own two eyes, I never would have believed it.

Love at first sight.

Whitt looked like he had been knocked on his ass.

Epilogue
Irish

As I held Coal and Adeline's little girl in my arms, I looked at my woman, who was smiling as Maisie told her a story about her day at school.

Yes, Maisie was now in school, and since that fucking bitch of a woman hadn't given a shit about Maisie, she was starting from scratch.

But every night, my woman worked with Maisie, and in no time, she knew all the letters of the alphabet, and she could count to fifty.

Which was why my heart broke for my woman.

We had been trying for months to have a baby together.

And last month, we finally broke down and went to see a doctor.

Sutton was infertile.

And there was no cure or treatment for it.

The doctor had given us options.

From having a surrogate to adopting.

But my woman, who was just as protective of me as I was of her, said, "I will be damned if another woman has any part of my man inside of her. One was fucking enough. And the possibility of other women is more than I could handle. Besides, I'm already a mother. Sure, I didn't give birth to her. But I've been in her life ever since she was five years old. That girl is mine. We don't need another child."

Then she looked at me, "Are you okay with that?"

"Made you a promise, baby. Give me all of your hopes and dreams, and I'll shelter you through any storm."

"But it's..." I placed my fingers over her lips.

"Long as I have you, then I'm golden. Went half of my life not having you and realized I wasn't living. Had you, I really lived. Then I lost you; I don't ever want to go through that again. So, what I'm trying to say is that I want what you want. And I always fucking will."

"Do I have you wrapped around my little pinky?" she asked in a teasing tone.

But I wasn't teasing when I nodded.

Because she did.

With her eyes.

Her cute little button nose.

The freckle on the side of her cheek.

The body she was gifted with.

That incredible brain of hers.

But most of all, it was her heart.

Her heart had ensnared my own. And made me forever hers.

And with the doctor dabbing at the corner of her eyes, we walked out of the office, her hand held tightly in mine, a smile on both of our faces.

We already had one hell of a family.

And it was perfect.

Sutton

Nine Years Later

I looked at Maisie and smiled, "If a man doesn't cut the balls off of any man that dares to do you harm, then he's not a man."

"Ew, Mom, why would you ever say that to me."

I smiled, "Because your father is that kind of man."

It took her a moment, and then she gasped, "No. No, he didn't."

I shrugged, "I can neither confirm or deny."

She was silent for a moment until she asked, "Who was it?"

I locked eyes with my gorgeous girl, who had boys panting after her already, and she was only fifteen years old, dropped my tone and said, "The man who ordered me to be raped and then sat there and watched it happen."

Tears immediately hit her eyes and then fell down her cheeks, "Oh, momma."

Oh, my soft-hearted girl. I, too, would kill anyone that hardened her heart.

I smiled softly at my girl and said, "You're old enough now to know about this kind of thing. Your father and I can only shield you so far. So, right now, I want you to promise me something, okay?"

She nodded.

Her eyes shone with tears at what I told her, "I mean it. The man you give your heart to make sure he's worthy. And if you don't feel it right down to the tips of your toes, then don't give your heart to him. You wait. No matter how long that takes. Because our heart is the most precious gift we have to give, and it has to be handled with care."

She nodded, then stood and wrapped me in her arms, "I love you, Mom."

I wrapped her in mine and whispered in her hair, "I love you too, pretty girl."

Later that night, I had just climbed off of Irish after I rode him hard.

But he wasn't through with me.

Oh no, not my man, I was flipped onto my hands and knees, my face buried in the pillow as he pounded inside of me.

It was so, oh so good, even after all these years later.

He hit that spot just right, I clenched around him and let it all go.

He followed suit not even two minutes later.

After we both cleaned up, I curled into his body, my head went to his chest, but not before my lips pressed a kiss to my name that was on his chest.

Yes, Irish stayed true to his word.

We never saw Cynnamin again.

And I didn't care.

I know that made me a bad person, but still.

I couldn't stand the woman.

And yes, he never, and I mean, he never was cold to me, ever again.

If something bothered him, he told me.

And over the past several years, my man was finally able to say that he knew what love was and what it really meant.

Because I had shown him.

But that's not all I showed him.

See, I had done something for Cruz when I was there.

And he owed me a favor.

He kept his promise.

And I made sure that the piece of shit parents, that were Irish's, were swept from this planet.

That news was my first wedding anniversary present to my husband.

Irish's fingers were trailing through my hair when he whispered, "Smooth, baby. So, fucking smooth."

I lifted my head from his chest and asked, "What are you talking about?"

"What you said to our girl. You were spot on. And I hope I've always handled your heart with care after I fucked up like I did."

I smiled, "You did. Like a smooth whiskey."

The End.

Thank You

Thank you so much for reading Smooth As Whiskey. When I started the As If... trilogy, I hesitated to write their story.

It was going to rip my heart out, put it back together, stomp on it, and then glue the pieces back together with Elmer's school glue.

But I am so glad that these two amazing characters chose me to tell their love story.

I hope you enjoyed the ride. I know I definitely did.

And yes... almost every single male character that has been mentioned in this book, well, they are getting their own books.

XOXO, Tiffany

Other Works

Wrath MC

Mountain of Clearwater
Clearwater's Savior
Clearwater's Hope
Clearwater's Fire
Clearwater's Miracle
Clearwater's Treasure
Clearwater's Luck
Clearwater's Redemption
Christmas in Clearwater

Dogwood's Treasures
Dove's Life
Phoenix's Plight
Raven's Climb
Wren's Salvation
Lo's Wraith
Sparrow's Grace
Lark's Precious

DeLuca Empire
The Devil & The Siren
The Cleaner & The Princess
The Soldier & The Dancer

As If...
Cold As Ice
Dark As Coal
Smooth As Whiskey

Zagan MC
Asher (Sept 2024)

Willow Creek
Where Hearts Align
Where Hearts Connect (TBD)
Where Hearts Grow (TBD)
Where Hearts Mend (TBD)

Pinewood Lake
Rise
Empower

Strength (Nov 2024)

Armor (Nov 2024)

Charlotte U

Perfectly Imperfect

Imperfection is Beauty

Virgin Mary's

Old-Fashioned

Bottled Manhattan (TBD)

Gaelic Punch (TBD)

Novella's

Hotter Than Sin

Silver Treasure

Wrath Ink

Connect With Me

Facebook
https://www.facebook.com/author.tiffany.casper

Instagram
https://www.instagram.com/authortiffanycasper/

Goodreads
https://www.goodreads.com/author/show/19027352.Tiffany_Casper

Made in the USA
Middletown, DE
18 February 2025